"Something happens to a man when he's rejected by the woman he loves,"

Jess said. "It makes him keep wondering why."

Victoria turned to him and drew in a ragged breath that seared her lungs. "We both know you never loved me, Jess. So don't try to act like the injured soul."

A tense moment passed. "You don't know anything about me," he said softly. "You never did."

She swallowed, struggling to push down the tears that continued to scald her throat. "I know enough. I know that if you'd really wanted me, you wouldn't have let me go. You wouldn't have walked away. And you wouldn't have waited four years to come back."

"Maybe I was waiting for you to come to me."

Dear Reader,

As you take a break from raking those autumn leaves, you'll want to check out our latest Silhouette Special Edition novels! This month, we're thrilled to feature Stella Bagwell's *Should Have Been Her Child* (#1570), the first book in her new miniseries, MEN OF THE WEST. Stella writes that this series is full of "rough, tough cowboys, the strong bond of sibling love and the wide-open skies of the west. Mix those elements with a dash of intrigue, mayhem and a whole lot of romance and you get the Ketchum family!" And we can't wait to read their stories!

Next, Christine Rimmer brings us *The Marriage Medallion* (#1567), the third book in her VIKING BRIDES series, which is all about matrimonial destiny and solving secrets of the past. In Jodi O'Donnell's *The Rancher's Daughter* (#1568), part of popular series MONTANA MAVERICKS: THE KINGSLEYS, two unlikely soul mates are trapped in a cave…and find a way to stay warm. *Practice Makes Pregnant* (#1569) by Lois Faye Dyer, the fourth book in the MANHATTAN MULTIPLES series, tells the story of a night of passion and a very unexpected development between a handsome attorney and a bashful assistant. Will their marriage of convenience turn to everlasting love?

Patricia Kay will hook readers into an intricate family dynamic and heart-thumping romance in *Secrets of a Small Town* (#1571). And Karen Sandler's *Counting on a Cowboy* (#1572) is an engaging tale about a good-hearted teacher who finds love with a rancher and his young daughter. You won't want to miss this touching story!

Stay warm in this crisp weather with six complex and satisfying romances. And be sure to return next month for more emotional storytelling from Silhouette Special Edition!

Happy reading!

Gail Chasan
Senior Editor

Please address questions and book requests to:
Silhouette Reader Service
U.S.: 3010 Walden Ave., P.O. Box 1325, Buffalo, NY 14269
Canadian: P.O. Box 609, Fort Erie, Ont. L2A 5X3

Should Have Been Her Child

STELLA BAGWELL

SPECIAL EDITION™

Published by Silhouette Books

America's Publisher of Contemporary Romance

To my editor, Mary-Theresa Hussey,
an angel who keeps me on the right course.

And to all the editors I work with at Silhouette.
I love you all.

 SILHOUETTE BOOKS

ISBN 0-373-24570-X

SHOULD HAVE BEEN HER CHILD

Copyright © 2003 by Stella Bagwell

This edition published by arrangement with Harlequin Books S.A.

® and TM are trademarks of Harlequin Books S.A., used under license. Trademarks indicated with ® are registered in the United States Patent and Trademark Office, the Canadian Trade Marks Office and in other countries.

Visit Silhouette at www.eHarlequin.com

Printed in U.S.A.

Books by Stella Bagwell

STELLA BAGWELL

Recently, Stella and her husband of thirty years moved from the hills of Oklahoma to Seadrift, Texas, a sleepy little fishing town located on the coastal bend. Stella says it is a lovely place to let her imagination soar and to put the stories in her head down on paper. She and her husband have one son, Jason, who lives and teaches high school math in nearby Port Lavaca.

Dear Reader,

This new miniseries—MEN OF THE WEST—is something I've wanted to write for a long time, but other stories kept popping up for my immediate attention. Now, as I approach my fiftieth book for Silhouette, I'm finally getting to write about the Ketchum family and all of their friends. What a joy! There's nothing sexier than a man in a pair of cowboy boots and hat. And when he's a lawman, too, well, he's pretty nigh irresistible to me.

There is an old saying that everything changes. But thankfully, in my case, I can say that isn't entirely true. Well, okay, I've aged a little. Yet as an author, the excitement and love I have for writing romance is still just as great as it was eighteen years ago when I sold my first story to Silhouette.

Being part of the Silhouette family has been a wonderful honor for me and I'd like to take this opportunity to thank all the editors I've worked with down through the years. You've made my job a pure pleasure! And last, but certainly not least, I'd like to thank you, all my loyal readers for buying my books. Without you, this job of mine wouldn't mean anything and I sincerely hope that I've given you as much pleasure reading my stories as I've gotten from creating them. And it's my fervent wish that you're as eager to read my next fifty books as I am to write them!

Thank you all from the bottom of my heart!

God bless,

Stella Bagwell

Chapter One

"Victoria, something has happened out at the T Bar K!"

The woman with dark hair sitting behind the large desk didn't bother lifting her head from the notes she was studying. "Something is always happening at the ranch. If he's bleeding, put him in exam room one. If he thinks something might be broken, take him on down to X ray and I'll be there in just a moment."

"No, Victoria. There's not an injured cowboy in the waiting room. It's something else."

Dr. Victoria Ketchum glanced up from the file on her desk to see her nurse's face peering around the edge of the office door.

Nevada Ortiz was usually unflappable. Even when patients were bleeding all over the floor or passing out in the waiting room. But right now the young woman's creamed-coffee complexion was downright pasty.

"What do you mean? Has some of my family called the clinic?"

Nevada quickly stepped inside the small office and approached Victoria's desk. "No. One of the patients was listening to his scanner and overheard the sheriff's department dispatching some men out there."

Like Nevada, Victoria had never been one to panic. Doctors simply couldn't allow themselves the luxury of losing their cool under fire. Now years of training and self-discipline surfaced to keep her pulse at an even pace and her thoughts focused toward a logical explanation.

"It isn't like you to listen to patients' gossip, Nevada."

The young nurse gave her boss a rueful smile. "You're right. If I stopped to listen to all the gossip that goes through this clinic I'd never get any work done. But I think this time there's something to it. You...haven't heard from the ranch in the past hour or so?"

Victoria shook her dark head. "No. And I'd be the first one my brother Ross would call if there'd been a severe accident or an injury. So that tells me no one has been injured." She closed the manila folder and rose from her chair. "Is Mr. Valdez still in exam room two?"

Nevada stepped back as her boss quickly moved from behind the massive oak desk. "Yes. But, Victoria, aren't you going to at least make a quick call to the ranch?" she asked with amazement. "If the law is headed out there...something must be happening."

Victoria's soft lips tilted into an indulgent smile for her nurse and friend. "They probably found the stud that's been missing for the past couple of weeks. And if that's the case, everyone on the ranch will have reason to celebrate tonight." She motioned for Nevada to join her as she headed out of the room. "Quit worrying and follow me. If I'm not mistaken, I still have three more patients to see before quitting time. We have work to do."

For the next hour, Victoria put any thoughts of the T Bar K out of her mind as she listened to aches and complaints and wrote down orders and prescriptions. Even though she was a Ketchum and still lived on the ranch, she was a doctor first and foremost and her patients' welfare was something she always put before herself.

But later that evening, after she'd left the clinic and headed her vehicle north out of Aztec, a strange sense of dread gnawed at the pit of her stomach. In all likelihood, the law had gone to the T Bar K to talk to her brother about the missing stallion. She couldn't imagine them going to the ranch for any other reason. Yet something like that wouldn't be considered an emergency requiring radio dispatch, she silently reasoned.

Don't borrow trouble, she scolded herself as she forced her fingers to relax on the steering wheel. For all she knew her nosy patient might have gotten his information mixed up. And anyway, even if men from the sheriff's department had visited the ranch, that didn't mean Jess had been one of them.

No, Jess Hastings, the undersheriff of San Juan County, probably had much more important things on his docket than to travel out to the home of an old flame.

Old flame. Dear Lord, how could she think of herself in those terms, she wondered. Jess has been out of her life for four years or more now. She was nothing to him. And obviously never had been.

After traveling several miles, she turned off the highway and onto a graveled road leading east into the high desert mountains.

May had brought much warmer weather to northern New Mexico. The snows in the higher elevations had started to melt, flooding the streams and rivers below. The Animas River, which cut through a section of the T Bar K, lay to the left of the winding dirt road. Now and then Victoria caught sight of the rushing rapids as her vehicle began the climb that would eventually take her to the ranch house.

When she finally entered the main gate leading up to the rambling log structure, the spring sun had already slid behind the mountains. Dusky purple shadows shrouded the house, which was perched on a ledge high enough to give a partial view of the valley floor below. Ketchum land. Farther than the eye could see.

But at the moment, Victoria wasn't seeing anything except the two utility vehicles with official markings of the San Juan County sheriff's department parked a few feet from the rail fence running in front of the house.

So Nevada's warning had been right, she thought, as she deliberately drove around to the back entrance of the house. Something had happened. She could only pray it wasn't something bad. The Ketchum family had already had their share of bad this past year. What with Tucker dying, a drought putting a heavy financial strain on the ranch and then the stud's disappearance, she could hardly imagine getting more wretched news.

As always, the long kitchen was warm and filled with the spicy scents of waiting supper. At the huge gas range, the cook, Marina, glanced over her shoulder as Victoria's footsteps tapped across the tiled floor.

"Better not go to living room, *chica*. There's a powwow goin' on," the older woman warned.

Biting back a sigh, Victoria reached up and slipped the clasp from her hair to allow the thick black chocolate waves to tumble down around her shoulders. As she massaged her scalp, she reached for a glass in the cupboard.

"I saw the vehicles parked out front. What sort of powwow is going on? Has the stallion been found?"

Marina's chuckles were mocking as she pushed a wooden spoon through a pot of bubbling cheese sauce. "Somethin' has been found. But it no horse, *chica*."

Victoria paused anxiously as she pushed the glass under the tap. "What? How long has the law been here anyway?"

Marina put down her spoon and looked at Victoria. The Mexican woman had worked for the ranch longer than Victoria could remember. She was always jolly, gentle and compassionate. And now that Tucker and Amelia were gone, she was the last of the old ones. Though she wasn't an educated woman, and spoke only broken English, Victoria respected her wisdom just the same.

"Three hours, maybe. I was about—"

Marina's words stopped abruptly as the sound of someone entering the kitchen caught the attention of both women.

Victoria glanced around the cook's shoulder and immediately went stone still at the sight of Jess Hastings sauntering into the room. Even though he was dressed in blue jeans and a long-sleeved white shirt, the gun strapped to his hip and the badge on his chest told her he was on duty.

The moment he spotted her his mouth tightened, his eyes narrowed. Yet even from a distance she could see the span of four years hadn't changed him all that much. He was still long, lean and sinfully male. And suddenly her heart was racing like a wild animal caught in a deadly trap.

Thankfully, Marina wasn't as affected by the man. With one hand on her ample hip, she turned to face him. "You lost?"

Ignoring the cook's sarcasm, he inclined his head toward Victoria.

"I'd like to speak with Ms. Ketchum. Alone."

Dear Lord, how many times had she tried to forget that voice? The way it roughened with passion or softened like velvet. There was just a hint of a drawl in it now, reminding Victoria he'd been living near El Paso for the past four years.

She took a step toward him and forced herself to speak. "Marina is busy with supper. We can talk in the study."

He nodded and she walked briskly past him, out of the kitchen and down a long, dim hallway which led to the east wing of the house.

Even without the sound of his boots making contact

with the polished pine floor, Victoria would have known he was following. She could feel his presence behind her. Big, masculine, menacing.

Once inside the study, she switched on a table lamp, took a deep breath, then turned to face him.

"What's this all about?" she asked without preamble.

His lips twisted and once again her gaze zeroed in on achingly familiar features. The square jaw, jutted chin and eyes as gray as an angry thundercloud. He was not a handsome man. He was simply all male. Rough. Tough. And oh, so irresistible. She'd never wanted any man the way she'd wanted this one. And since him, she hadn't wanted any.

"I should have known there would be no 'hello, Jess,' or 'how are you doing, Jess?'"

The directness of his stare dared her to look away from him. Victoria's chin lifted ever so slightly at the challenge.

"I didn't expect you to want a greeting from me," she said.

He moved toward her and didn't stop until there was only the width of his hand separating the two of them. "I expect common courtesy from everyone. Including you Ketchums."

Her blood was pumping through her veins at such a high rate she actually felt light-headed. It was all she could do to stop herself from grabbing the front of his starched shirt just to keep herself from swaying.

"I didn't hear you asking about my well-being," she retorted.

His eyes took their slow, easy time slipping over her long dark hair, soft white skin, blue-green eyes and full red lips. She was as gorgeous as he remembered. Maybe even more so, if that was possible.

For four years he'd tried to forget the image of this woman. How she'd felt in his arms and in his bed. For a while he'd believed that given time he'd be able to exorcise her from his mind. And there were days when he did manage to shake her memory for a few hours. Then she was always back, haunting his past, spoiling his future.

"Hello, Victoria. How are you?"

The softly spoken question was not what she'd been expecting. Even as her senses scattered, she struggled not to let him see what she was thinking. Feeling. Seeing him again shouldn't be doing this to her. But damn it, Jess Hastings was the one and only thing that could unsettle her.

"If you really want to know, I was fine until I heard that lawmen had invaded the T Bar K."

One corner of his mouth tilted upward into a semblance of a smile. "I wouldn't call it an invasion. There's only two of us here. Myself and Deputy Redwing."

She desperately needed to turn and walk away. To put a few feet between them so that she could breathe without drawing in his seductive scent, so that she could look at anything other than his chiseled lips and damning eyes. But where she was concerned, Jess had always been a magnet. She couldn't move away. Not just yet.

"So you're the undersheriff now," she said softly. "What happened to your job with the border patrol?"

The grooves bracketing his lips deepened with a tight grimace. "I resigned. For personal reasons."

Even though Victoria was in an occupation that exposed her to many people and even more gossip, she'd never heard anyone say why Jess Hastings had returned to San Juan County four months ago. And she'd not been brave enough to ask. But now the question was on the tip of her tongue, making her bite down to keep the words from passing her lips.

"How's your medical practice?" he asked.

"Very busy."

Her short answer told him she didn't want to discuss her life with him. Which didn't surprise Jess. She'd stopped wanting to share anything with him a long time ago.

"I guess you're wanting to know what I'm doing here?"

She nodded once. "It would help."

To her surprise, he took hold of her upper arm and led her to a nearby leather couch. Before she sank onto one of the cushions she was struck with the fact of how mushy her knees had grown and how her arm burned where he touched her.

Easing down beside her, Jess pulled off his Stetson and combed his fingers through his short, sandy hair.

"I suppose you know the ranch hands have been out searching for Ross's stallion," he began.

"Yes. But Marina informed me that he hasn't been found."

Jess stroked his fingers along one side of his jaw as he studied her waiting eyes.

"No. The men found something else," he said grimly. "A body."

She wanted to gasp, but the air was suddenly

trapped in her lungs. She shook her head, then shook it again. "Did you say a body?"

He continued to search her face. "That's right. Partially decomposed. But enough to tell us it was human and we think male."

"Oh dear Lord," she whispered. "Who—"

"I've been questioning your family and some of the hands on the ranch," he answered her unfinished question. "No one seems to have any idea of who this person might have been or why he was on the T Bar K. I was hoping you might be able to tell me something."

Incredulous, her gaze latched on to his. "Me? How could I know anything?"

One sandy brow lifted sardonically. "You live here, too."

"Yes, but I don't know—" She stopped, her eyes narrowing suspiciously. "This body—are you—do you think there was foul play involved or someone just came along and died of natural causes or an accident?"

His thumb and forefinger slid along the brim of his hat, flattening any bumps or dips from the expensive felt. She tried not to notice his big hands or remember the pleasure they used to give her.

"You're a doctor. You know it takes time to determine those sorts of things."

She drew in a needy breath, then slowly released it. "Yes. But—there might have been clues—"

His smile was slow and a bit too indulgent for Victoria's liking. But then, she didn't want Jess Hastings to smile at her in any way or for any reason. He was a silver-tongued wolf who'd gobbled up her heart, then spit out the pieces.

"Those are to be shared with the sheriff's department," he said shortly. "Not the Ketchum family."

She wanted to stand and walk away from him, but she was afraid her legs wouldn't hold her, so she stayed where she was and tried to hold her temper in check. Crossing words with Jess would get her nowhere.

"Well, I'm sorry, but there's nothing I can tell you."

"You might be surprised about that," he said quietly.

She tried not to shiver as a strange chill traveled down her spine. "You can't think I would know anything about this person."

His expression didn't change. "Oh, I don't know. I have a habit of thinking things I shouldn't. Has anyone made you angry in the past few months? So angry that you wanted to kill him?"

She stared at him in stunned fascination. "You're kidding."

His gray eyes didn't blink. "Finding a body is nothing to kid about."

And she could see that he was serious. Fear, then anger poured though her body, making her go cold, then hot. "You just told me you didn't know if foul play was involved or not. So why do you want to know if anyone has angered me to the extent of committing murder?"

He smiled, but there was no humor behind the curve of his lips. "You always were a little too sharp for me. Weren't you, Tori?"

"Don't call me that!" she whispered icily. He was the only person who'd ever called her by that nickname and as far as she was concerned he'd lost his right to be that intimate with her. "And as for your question, no one has angered me in the past months. But a few years ago—I could have killed you. Given the chance," she added.

Jess was a man known for keeping his head. It was one of the reasons he'd excelled at his job. A man with a cool head didn't miss anything going on around him. He could reason, stay aware and stay alive. But there had always been something about Victoria that heated his blood. And it wasn't just the lush, feminine shape of her. One glance, one word from her had the power to ignite an explosion in him. And she'd just set him off.

He said, "I guess Ketchum blood must be stronger than that Hippocratic oath you took."

She was shocked to see her fingers had clenched, forming fists at her sides. She forced her hands to relax and her lungs to breathe. "What is that supposed to mean?"

His gray eyes slipped downward to where her breasts pushed against pale blue cashmere. The fabric was as soft as her skin and a knot twisted in his gut at the memory of her full breasts cupped in his hands, the rosy brown nipples begging to be kissed.

He looked at the floor, then back up to her face. "The oath is to save lives, not take them. But—where I'm concerned you only see me through Ketchum eyes."

"My family never disliked you."

He let out a harsh laugh, then rose to his feet and

crossed the room to where a low fire crackled and spit in a native rock fireplace. "Tucker couldn't stand the thought of you being anywhere near me."

She wanted to point out that his comments had nothing to do with his visit to the T Bar K this evening, but she didn't. For the past four months, since she'd heard Jess had come back to San Juan county, she'd known a time would come when she would have to face him again, to discover for herself if he held any bitterness about the past. She didn't have to wonder anymore.

"My father didn't try to prevent me from seeing you."

His head turned away from the fire to stab her with a hot glare. "Not in words. No, the old man was too sly for that. He knew just how to get to you. And he did."

Her jaw clenched. "I thought four years would have made you see how wrong you were. But it's obvious you're still just as blind and bullheaded as you ever were!"

"You're the blind one, Victoria. You were then. And you are now."

If he'd spoken the words in anger she would have understood them. But there had been no animosity in his voice. Just a quiet sort of warning.

Before she realized what she was doing, she left the couch and went to stand in front of him. "Is that supposed to mean something?"

He took a deep breath, then reached for a small framed photo on the fireplace mantel. It was a snapshot of Tucker and Amelia in their younger days, back when their four children had been small and the oldest, Hugh, had still been alive.

"Everybody but you knows Tucker Ketchum was a shady character—"

"You don't—"

"That's one of the reasons why this ranch is so big and profitable. And I'm afraid it's a likely reason a body was discovered facedown in an arroyo on the T Bar K."

She pushed at the heavy wave of nearly black hair dipping over her eye. "You're despicable! You're not fit to be this county's undersheriff."

"Why? Because I didn't hang around and let the old man corrupt me, too?"

Raw fury brought her hand up and swinging at his face. He caught her wrist easily and jerked her up against him.

"This whole thing is making you happy, isn't it?" She flung the question at him. "You've just been waiting for some reason to spite my family. And now you have it in the form of a dead body!"

His arm slipped around her back to still her squirms. "Nothing about this is making me happy, Victoria." His eyes suddenly focused on her lips and then his head bent. "Especially not this."

A kiss was the last thing she'd expected from the man and for a moment she was frozen with shock at the feel of his hard lips spreading over hers. Then her hands lifted to his broad shoulders and pushed. The feeble gesture of disapproval caused his lips to ease a fraction away from hers. But his hold on her back tightened, making her breasts flatten against him, her hips arch into his.

"Jess—"

If she had whispered his name in protest, he would have released her. But there had only been hunger in the sound of her voice and his desire fed on it like flames to the wind.

Time ceased to exist as his lips searched the sweetness of her mouth, his hands roamed the warmth of her back, then tangled in the thick waves of her hair.

Long before he lifted his head, she was clutching folds of his shirt, struggling to keep her knees from buckling. Her breathing was ragged, her heart racing like a wild horse on a lightning-struck mesa. No one but Jess could make her feel so helpless, so alive. So much a woman.

Dear Lord, nothing had changed, she thought desperately. Four long, lonely years had done nothing to erase this man from her heart.

"Is this how you question your female suspects nowadays?" she finally managed to ask.

Slowly, he moved his arm from around her back and she quickly put several inches between the two of them.

"That wasn't a question, Tori. That was a statement."

She swallowed as she pressed the back of her hand against her burning lips. "The statement being?"

He smiled, but once again there was no warmth or sincerity behind the expression.

"That I'm in charge of things now. And the fact that you're a Ketchum means nothing where the law is concerned."

Pain splintered in the middle of her chest, but she somehow met his gaze in spite of it.

"Is that how you kissed me? As a lawman? Or the Jess I used to know?"

For long moments his gray eyes simply roamed her flushed face. Then his lips parted, but before he could reply, a knock interrupted him.

Glancing over her shoulder, Victoria saw a young Native American man dressed similarly to Jess standing in the open doorway of the study. Victoria noticed that his dark, curious glance missed nothing as he took in the sight of her and Jess standing close together on the hearth.

"Sorry to interrupt, Jess. I thought you'd want to know the head wrangler has arrived back on the ranch. He's waiting in the bunkhouse."

The head wrangler for the T Bar K was Linc Ketchum, Victoria's cousin. Like the rest of her family, she seriously doubted he would have any answers for the lawmen.

"I'll be right there, Redwing," Jess told him.

Nodding, the deputy slipped from view. Beside her, Jess made a move to leave the room. Before he could walk away, she reached out and caught his arm.

One brow arched with mocking inquisition as he paused and glanced down at her.

"Jess, what does this all mean?"

The quiet desperation in her voice was a spur in his ribs, both painful and irritating. "We'll just have to see, now won't we, Tori?"

Chilled by his sarcasm, she dropped her hand from his arm. "You're not the same man I used to know, Jess."

His lips thinned, his nostrils flared as the track of his gray eyes burned her face. "No. I'll never be that man again."

Chapter Two

The night air had grown chilly and mosquitoes were making a feast of her bared forearms, but Victoria was loath to move from her spot on the patio to return inside the house.

Jess and his deputy had left the ranch more than two hours ago, yet the place was still buzzing—*she* was still buzzing. And she didn't like it.

She hadn't thought that seeing Jess again would have left her this shaken. And she tried to tell herself it was the circumstances of his appearance that were the real reason she was so disturbed. After all, it wasn't every day a body was discovered on her family's land, without any sort of explanation as to why or how it had gotten there.

"Victoria? I wondered where you'd gotten to."

From her chair, she glanced over her shoulder at

her brother Ross, then back out to the dark, pine-covered mountain rising like a sentinel over the T Bar K ranch house.

"For the past hour I've been trying to muster up enough energy to leave this chair," she told him.

His hand came down on her shoulder and gently squeezed. "You hardly ate any supper. Are you feeling all right?"

She tried to laugh, but the sound held little cheer. "Remember, I'm the doctor, Ross. I'm supposed to ask that question."

He eased his long frame down in the woven lawn chair sitting at an angle to hers. "That's the trouble with you, Victoria. You're always taking care of others rather than yourself."

At thirty-five, and five years older than Victoria, Ross was the younger Ketchum son. Since their brother Hugh had been killed in an accident with a bull six years ago, Ross had taken total reins of managing the T Bar K. Along with being business savvy, Ross was as handsome as sin and some said as tough as their late father, Tucker. But to Victoria he was always gentle, her rock when no one else was there for her.

Casting him a wan smile, she said, "I'm all right, Ross. It's just been a…long day."

He sighed. "A hell of a long day," he agreed.

"Were you able to contact Seth?"

"No. He's out. On a case, more than likely."

Their older brother Seth had moved away from the ranch many years ago to become a Texas Ranger. If a problem did arise over the discovered body, Seth would know how to handle it. Victoria could only hope their older brother wouldn't have to be bothered.

"It's just as well. There's really not a problem. And I don't foresee one."

"How do you figure?" Ross asked.

She rubbed the mosquito bites on the back of her arm. "Obviously this man wandered onto Ketchum land and died of natural causes or suffered a fall for one reason or another. There's nothing sinister about that."

Ross thoughtfully stroked his chin. "I'm surprised you used that word. Jess didn't imply there was anything sinister going on."

Her mind whirled as she regarded her brother's rugged face. "That's not the impression he gave me."

Ross's brows lifted. "Maybe you misread the man."

"The only time I misread Jess Hastings was four years ago. When he left San Juan County."

But tonight Victoria had read him loud and clear. Especially his kiss. He was out to hurt her, any way he could. And the idea left a terrible ache in her heart.

"Hell, Victoria," her brother gently scolded, "I thought you'd gotten Jess Hastings out of your system a long time ago."

She rose to her feet with plans to go back inside. "I have. I just haven't forgotten the hard lesson he taught me."

He studied her for long moments. "I hope you had the good sense not to anger the man, Victoria. He's in a position to help us or hurt us. I wouldn't want it to be the latter."

It didn't dawn on Ross that Jess had already hurt

her more than anything or anyone ever could. But then Ross didn't know the whole story behind her and Jess. No one did. And as far as she was concerned, no one ever would.

"If Jess decides to pursue this thing in a negative way, there's nothing I can do to stop him," she said, then hurried inside the house before her brother could say more.

The baby-fine curls surrounded the child's head like a red-gold halo. Long curling lashes of the same color lay against cheeks flushed from the warmth of the nearby fireplace.

Jess's daughter had been asleep in his arms for some time now, but still he lingered in the rocker, savoring the feel of her warm weight resting against his chest. She was the only thing he'd done right in his life. The only thing he really lived for. Her and his grandparents.

"Is Katrina asleep? I've got your supper heated in the microwave."

Jess looked up from his daughter's face to see Alice, his grandmother, standing a few steps away in the dimly lit living room. She was a tall, rawboned woman, her skin brown and wrinkled by hard work and nearly seventy years of harsh, New Mexico climate. Her hands were big and tough, her hair gray and wiry. But her heart was as gentle as a Chinook wind that melted the winter snows.

When Jess's father had died at an early age from pneumonia complicated by alcoholism, he'd left behind a five-year-old son and a wife who'd never really wanted a husband and child in the first place. As soon as Jim Hastings had been planted in the ground, his wife had left for greener pastures.

Thankfully, Alice and William had been there to take in their grandson and raise him as their own child. Ma and Pa, as Jess called them, were the only real parents he'd ever known. And now they were helping him raise his own daughter. But they were getting too old to see after a rambunctious two-and-a-half-year-old toddler, even if Jess did take her into a day care near Cedar Hill for most of the day.

"Yeah, she's asleep. I've just been holding her. Thinking how much she's grown since the two of us came home to the ranch."

Alice smiled with affection as she took in the sight of her grandson and great-granddaughter. "She's really starting to string her words together now. But Pa had to scold her for saying a curse word today."

Jess chuckled. "Now I wonder where she might have heard such a thing?" he asked as he carefully rose from the rocker with the toddler still cradled in his arms.

"Pa said it was from me," Alice said. "But we both know I've never said a bad word in my life."

"Only if you were by yourself or with someone else," Jess joked.

Alice's laughter followed him as he carried his daughter down a narrow hallway and into a small bedroom situated next to his.

After placing her in a white, wooden crib, he made certain she was covered against the night chill, then headed back through the old house to the kitchen.

Even though the hour was late and Will had gone

to bed two hours earlier, his grandmother was there waiting for him.

"You didn't have to wait for me, Ma. I can fend for myself," he assured her. But already she'd placed his plate of food on the table, along with silverware and a tall glass of iced tea.

Waving away his words, she sank down in the chair next to him and pushed a hand through her gray hair.

"I'll go to bed in a minute. I wanted to ask you what happened today out at the T Bar K."

Shaking black pepper over the food, Jess paused to look at her. "News sure does travel fast for us to be living fifteen miles from town. It's not like you to be gossiping on the telephone."

"Who has time for the damn telephone? I went into Aztec for a few things at the grocery. Ed mentioned it when I checked out."

Jess shoveled a bite of black beans into his mouth. "What makes you think I know anything about it?"

She made a face at him. "You're the undersheriff," she said proudly. "If anything of importance happens around here, you're gonna know it."

With a wry shake of his head, Jess said, "A body was discovered on T Bar K range."

"I've heard that much."

He chewed a forkful of rice spiced with chili peppers. "There's not much more to tell. We'll have to wait and see what the coroner uncovers."

Alice sighed. "I guess…what I was really wondering was…if you saw Victoria while you were at the ranch."

He glanced up to see his grandmother regarding him with quiet concern. Since he'd returned from

Texas, she'd not brought up the subject of Victoria. Not that there was anything to bring up. That part of his life had been over for years now. He'd already married and lost a wife since Victoria had turned her back on him.

"Why would you want to know that?" he hedged.

Impatient now, she asked, "Well, did you?"

His gaze slipped back to his plate. "Yeah. I questioned her."

Surprise crossed her wrinkled face. "Questioned her? Why?"

"Ma," he said tiredly, "it's my job."

Moments passed as Jess continued to eat.

Finally, Alice asked, "So was she…glad to see you?"

Jess gripped his fork as he thought about the impulsive kiss he'd exchanged with Victoria. For a few seconds her lips had said she was glad to have him close again. But her words had conveyed something altogether different. And Jess wasn't ever going to repeat the mistake of allowing her body to rule his thinking.

"No person is ever glad to see a lawman, Ma. Unless they're in trouble and need help."

Rising from her chair, Alice crossed to a large gas range and turned the flame under a red granite coffeepot.

"Did you ever stop to think Victoria fits that bill?"

He snorted. "Victoria is a Ketchum. They have money and power. And now that she's a practicing physician, she has even more money to buy herself out of anything."

Alice shot him a disgusted look as she pulled a mug

down from a pine cupboard. "I'm not talking about trouble with the law, Jess."

His fork paused in midair as he glanced at his grandmother. "What are you talking about, Ma?"

She poured the coffee, then placed it next to his right hand. "I think you need to figure that out for yourself."

Jess realized there wasn't any point asking her what she meant by that comment. She was already on her way out of the kitchen. And even if she hadn't been headed to bed, she wouldn't have explained. She'd always liked to let him stew in his own juices.

Well, it won't work this time, Ma, Jess said to himself. Victoria Ketchum was a bad memory from his past. And if she was in any sort of trouble, she'd have to look elsewhere for help. He wasn't about to become involved with the woman again. And from her reaction to him earlier this evening, she wasn't about to let him.

He finished his meal and the last of his coffee. After rinsing the dishes, he walked down to the barn. On the south side of the building two horses milled about in separate lots. Normally at this time of year the horses were loose and running the range, feasting on new spring grasses. Pa had kept the horses penned for more than a week now, waiting for Jess to find time to help him with roundup.

At seventy-one, Will was still spry and healthy and a better cowhand than most men thirty years younger. Jess didn't want to think about the time his grandfather would no longer be able to pitch hay, build fences or brand cattle. As for riding a horse, the old man would be happy to die in the saddle.

Jess checked the watering troughs and feed buckets hanging on the rail fence even though he knew Will had already seen to the horses' needs. He was simply making the rounds, satisfying the lawman inside of him that all was well.

In the morning, he would tell Pa to give him two or three more days and then he'd help him hit the brush. Since there was only the two of them, it would take at least three days of hard riding to scour the mountains and arroyos around the ranch for stray Hastings cattle.

They didn't have a bunkhouse full of cowboys to do the work for them. But even if he had those resources, Will wouldn't want it that way. Like Jess, the old man was a proud loner. He didn't want anyone doing his job for him. Yet he welcomed Jess's companionship and helping hand, because Jess was family. And someday all of this would be his grandson's.

For the past four years Jess's help in keeping the Hastings ranch going had been in the form of money. A part of the salary he'd earned with the border patrol. And if Katrina's mother hadn't been killed in a car accident, he supposed he would have still been in El Paso.

Sighing wearily, he lifted the felt hat from his head and scraped his fingers through thick waves flattened against his skull.

It must be true that all things happened for a reason, he thought, as he walked slowly back toward the small, stucco house. Regina hadn't been the love of his life. He'd married her believing she would fill the empty hole in him after Victoria had rejected him. But she hadn't. And he supposed he couldn't blame her for divorcing him. He hadn't been able to give her his heart or the richer lifestyle she'd so dreamed about.

Her untimely death had left his little girl without a mother. Yet it had brought him back to New Mexico, to his grandparents and a job that was better suited to him.

Yes, he thought, all things happened for a reason. Some good. Some bad. Now he could only wonder what this trouble at the T Bar K was going to mean. For him. And the Ketchums.

Victoria had reached the end of her rope. Rather than discussing their health problems, three-quarters of her patients preferred to hear the scoop about the body found on the T Bar K. Who was it? What had happened? What was the law doing about it? Was the sheriff's department calling it a murder?

She couldn't get any work done, much less find a moment of peace to clear her mind. By six o'clock on the fourth evening after Jess's visit to the ranch, she was ready to scream.

Her jagged nerves must have shown on her face when Nevada rapped lightly on the open door of her office.

"Knock, knock. Is it safe to come in?"

Victoria frowned at the young nurse. "Since when have you ever worried about entering my office?"

"About two minutes ago. You looked as though you could wring someone's neck."

Victoria signed her name to the bottom of the document she'd been reading, then slapped the paper atop a pile she'd been meaning to clear from her desk for two days. "It's been a difficult day," she tried to explain.

Nevada eased her hip onto the corner of the desk. "You look exhausted."

Victoria chuckled. "I'm not twenty-two like you, Nevada. I'm thirty. By six in the evening I look wilted."

Nevada shook a finger at her. "That's not your age. That's from working too hard."

"I'm not the only one who works hard around here." She gave the nurse a grateful smile. "Has Lois already gone home?"

Nevada nodded. "The receptionist is gone, the front door is locked and the lights are out. You should be leaving, too."

Victoria rose from the leather chair and began to gather several medical reports she planned to read tonight.

Nevada kept her seat, seemingly not in any hurry to leave Victoria. It wasn't like the young woman, Victoria decided. Normally, she was always in a rush to get home or run some sort of errand, not to mention call one of her countless boyfriends.

"Uh—did you find something bad on Mrs. Barton's test results?"

Victoria gave her friend and co-worker a reassuring smile. "No. Mrs. Barton is going to be fine. The tests show her heart is strong and healthy. She strained a muscle in her chest while playing baseball with her ten-year-old son. The pain was mimicking angina, that's all."

"Oh, that's good news. I thought—well, you've looked a little down these past few days. I was afraid it might have something to do with one of the patients. You treat them all as if they were your family."

With Victoria's mother passing, her brother being killed and then her father dying, the past years had seen her once-large family dwindle down to only two brothers. To make up for the void, she supposed she had turned more and more to her patients.

"You worry too much about me, Nevada."

The younger woman shot Victoria an affectionate grin. "You're my boss. And friend. I'd rather see you smiling."

Victoria made a motion that the two of them should leave the small office. After turning off the light, the women walked slowly down a narrow hallway which would lead them to a back exit of the brick building that served as Victoria's private clinic.

As they walked, Victoria replied, "It's hard for me to smile when all I hear is questions and speculations about a body being found on the ranch. I'm really getting weary of people asking me about it."

Shrugging, Nevada reasoned, "It's big news, Victoria. The whole thing has aroused curiosity in the community. That's only natural."

"I understand that much. But it's impossible to discuss medications, treatments or health problems when my patients want to gossip."

Nevada had to laugh. "I know what you mean. I can hardly take a blood pressure without people bombarding me with questions. Maybe the authorities will come up with some new information that will quieten down all this talk."

Victoria nodded hopefully. "What's needed is a concrete explanation. One that will satisfy all this curiosity and all the townsfolk will turn their attention elsewhere.''

Reaching the back door, the two women paused.

''You're right about needing an explanation,'' Nevada agreed. ''But how long do you think it's going to take the law to figure things out? Sometimes these unknown identity cases take months, even years, before they're solved.''

Victoria groaned at the thought. Several months of this and she'd pull out her hair. ''I can't stand another *week* of this uproar, much less months. I've got to do something about it.''

Interest peaked Nevada's dark brows. ''Like what?'' she asked eagerly.

''Once I leave here, I'm going over to the sheriff's department,'' Victoria stated firmly. ''I want answers. Or if not answers, at least some reassurance that the law is moving on this case.''

A wicked grin suddenly appeared on Nevada's pretty face. ''Hmmm. You might meet up with some resistance there,'' she said.

Victoria knew the younger woman was talking about Jess. Although she hadn't known the nurse before the undersheriff had left the area and Victoria behind, Nevada had heard about their relationship. At least, what the general public knew about it and the bits that Victoria had volunteered to her. But she'd not told the other woman everything. No one, not even her family members, knew how much she had loved Jess Hastings or the devastation his leaving had caused her. She'd kept most of it hidden. After all, she was a doctor. She couldn't be needy herself. She had to take care of the needy.

"I didn't say I was going over there to see Jess," Victoria pointed out. "There are other officers in the department, including the sheriff."

Nevada shook her head. "I heard Sheriff Perez is in Santa Fe on some sort of conference. You won't be talking to him."

Victoria refused to be deterred. Tomorrow when her patients started in about John Doe's body, she was going to have some sort of information to put their curiosity to rest. "Then I'll see Deputy Redwing," she told Nevada. "He was at the ranch with Jess, so he's obviously working the case."

Nevada's black eyes suddenly glinted with interest at the mention of the young Native American lawman. "I wouldn't mind talking to him myself," she purred.

Groaning, Victoria reached for the door. "I know you're having fun playing the field now. But eventually your heart is going to be broken and when it is, you'll be wishing you never heard the word *'man.'*"

Nevada chuckled. "Sometimes a girl has to take a chance, Victoria."

"Hmm. Well, I'm all finished with taking chances. I'll leave that up to you, Nevada. But when you find yourself trying to glue the pieces of your heart back together, you'll know what I'm talking about."

Minutes later as Victoria headed across town she began to doubt her decision to visit the sheriff's office. Sticking her nose further into the investigation would probably only make matters worse. From his attitude the other day, Jess would like nothing better than to deal her a pile of misery. More than he already had, she thought grimly.

But this whole matter was interfering with her work. And she wasn't about to let anything come between her and her patients. Even Jess Hastings.

After parking in the first available space near the sheriff's office, she pulled off her lab coat, then glanced hurriedly in the rearview mirror. Except for a few loose tendrils, her dark hair was still pulled in a loose knot of curls atop her head.

She smoothed back a stray wisp from her forehead, but stopped short of applying powder or lipstick. If she did happen to run into Jess, she didn't want him thinking she'd spruced up for his benefit or any of the other law officers.

Inside the building she stopped at the first desk she came to. Seated behind it, a blond, middle-aged woman dressed in a police uniform was talking on the telephone.

Placing her hand over the receiver's mouthpiece, she questioned Victoria, "Can I help you with something?"

"I'm Victoria Ketchum," she explained. "I'd like to talk with Deputy Redwing if I could."

The woman shook her head. "Sorry. The deputy isn't in right now. Is there someone else—uh, did you say your name was Ketchum?"

Victoria didn't miss the sudden spark of recognition in the woman's eyes. "Yes. Dr. Victoria Ketchum. I wanted—"

"I think the lady wants to talk with me."

Both women turned their heads at the approaching male voice and Victoria's heart sped into overdrive at the sight of Jess striding her way.

Turning toward him, she said coolly, "I wouldn't want to take up your time, Officer Hastings."

The smile on his face matched the frost in her voice. "I'm sure what we have to talk about will only take a few minutes." He gestured for her to precede him down a short corridor. "Come along to my office."

She'd rather crawl into a rattlesnake den than join him in the privacy of his office. But with the other woman watching, she could hardly put up a fuss. Especially when she figured that even on a slack day it would be hard for anyone to get a word with Jess without an appointment.

As she walked past him, he told the woman officer, "Don't disturb me with any calls for the next few minutes, Sharon. I'll get any messages after I'm finished with Ms. Ketchum."

Finished with Ms. Ketchum. He was so right, Victoria thought grimly. He'd done that a long time ago. But as she followed him out of the room, she wondered why nothing between the two of them felt finished. Instead, she had the gnawing feeling it was starting all over again.

Chapter Three

Jess's office was located through a second door on the right of the large hallway. Somewhere, farther in the back of the building, Victoria could hear raised male voices, although she couldn't decipher the words being said. No doubt the muffled shouts were unhappy complaints from arrestees.

Across the hallway, several officers were grouped around a table littered with coffee and soft drink cups. Deputy Redwing was not among them, so the woman at the front desk must have been telling the truth about the man not being in the building. It would be her unfortunate luck that he was out and Jess was in, she thought dismally.

The room Jess ushered her into was small. Inside the cluttered space was a large desk with a comfortable leather chair, two tall file cabinets and, for visitors, a couple of straight-backed wooden chairs. Beneath a wide window on the south wall, a table held a coffeemaker and all the fixings. Atop one of the file cabinets, a radio was playing at a very low volume. After a moment she realized it was tuned to a local country station.

Closing the door behind him, he said, "Have a seat, Victoria."

It was more of a command than an invitation. She decided to ignore it and stand.

"I don't want to—take up that much of your time," she reasoned.

"You've already said that." While he eased his long frame into the leather chair behind his desk, he gestured for her to do his bidding. "So why don't you let me be the one to worry about my time?"

She was on his turf now. If she tried to resist him too much, she'd only wind up making a fool out of herself, she decided. And it probably would be better to take Jess sitting down. He'd always had a bad habit of weakening her knees.

"Now," he said after she'd made herself comfortable on the wooden chair. "What were you wanting to see Deputy Redwing about?"

Victoria forced herself to meet his gaze. And just like three days ago, she felt jolted all the way to her toes. "About the body, of course."

His gray eyes flicked keenly over her face, then dropped to her thin yellow sweater and on down to where her crossed legs were exposed by the slit in her brown skirt. He was the only man who knew what she looked like beneath her clothing and she could only hope that time had dimmed his memory.

''What about it?'' he asked.

She released an impatient breath. ''What's happening in the investigation? Have you found out anything?''

Crossing his arms across his chest, Jess leaned back in the chair and continued to study her for several long seconds. ''Funny, you didn't think there was anything to get in a stew about a few days ago when we found the body. Now you're wanting answers.''

Her nostrils flared as she tried to hold on to her temper. Back in the days when she and Jess were a couple, she'd not even possessed a temper. But then he'd never done anything to hurt or anger her. That hadn't happened until he'd gotten the wild idea to tear off to Texas.

''I still don't think there's anything...sinister about the man's death,'' she said. ''As a matter of fact, I'm not the one wanting the information. It's my patients.''

One brow arched with sarcasm. ''That's a good one, Victoria. Better than most I hear.''

His mocking attitude caused her lips to purse with disapproval. ''It's true, Jess. I can't—these past few days in my clinic have been—well, do you know what it's like trying to tell a man what he should be eating to lower his cholesterol while he's asking me what the sheriff's department is doing about the poor fella they found on the T Bar K?''

A bland smile crossed his features. ''I'm sure it's just as frustrating as people coming in here trying to tell me how to do my job.''

''But you have the choice of telling them to leave. I don't.''

His expression didn't soften. ''You have a mouth.

Use it. Explain that the poor fella who died on the T Bar K is none of their business. That should be easy enough.''

She passed a hand over her forehead and realized as she did that her fingers were trembling and beads of sweat had popped out on her skin.

Signs of fatigue, she told herself. Which shouldn't surprise her. She'd had little rest these past few nights. Sleep had come in fitful snatches while her dreams had been tortured with images of the man sitting across from her. She had to get a grip on herself. She couldn't go on like this.

''Twenty-five times a day?'' she asked dryly, then her eyes narrowed as something he'd just said struck her. ''You said the man who died on the T Bar K. Do you know for a fact that he died there? Or was he dumped on the ranch afterwards?''

Her questions caused him to lean forward and prop his elbows atop the desk. Even with several inches separating them, Victoria could feel his presence. Strong. Virile. And unyielding. Those things that had once attracted her to Jess were now the very things that unsettled her the most.

''If the body had been dumped, then there could only be one conclusion. And that would be murder. But, I was merely making conversation, not stating facts.'' He continued to regard her with mild suspicion. ''Why? Do you know something I don't?''

She made an impatient gesture with her hand. ''I came to you for answers, Jess. Not the other way around.''

''If I remember correctly, you came here to see

Deputy Redwing. That's what I heard you telling Sharon.''

He was playing cat and mouse with her. Teasing her with words and phrases when all along he knew every thought that was flitting through her head. Damn him.

"I did ask to see Deputy Redwing,'' she admitted. "I figured he'd be much easier to get answers from than you. And it looks as though I figured right.''

To her amazement, he chuckled. "Don't bet on it. Daniel is kinda like me. He likes to keep things under his hat. And he's very stubborn if anyone tries to persuade him otherwise. Including beautiful women.''

That last she desperately tried to ignore, but the foolish, feminine side of her couldn't help wondering if he really did think of her as beautiful. At one time she'd believed he had. He'd sworn she was everything to him.

The two of them had met by happenchance. She'd been finishing up the last of her internship at a Farmington hospital. During a drive home for the weekend a perfectly good tire had blown and very nearly caused her to wreck the car.

She'd been trying to lift the spare out of the trunk when a police car had pulled up behind her. The officer on duty had been Jess and the sight of his tall, muscular frame and rugged face had instantly bowled her over. While he'd changed the tire, he'd repeatedly called her Ms. Ketchum and she'd continually watched the strong muscles in his arms and shoulders ripple beneath his uniform as he strained to loosen and tighten lug nuts.

It had been Victoria who'd taken the initiative and

suggested they should get together later, when he wasn't posing as a lawman. He'd laughed and told her he wasn't posing. He *was* a lawman. And always would be.

After that day, the two of them had become almost inseparable. The attraction between them had been instant and fiery. She'd wanted to spend every spare minute with him and he with her. Suddenly her plans to simply be a small-town doctor had changed to a small-town doctor with a family. As for Jess, he'd sworn she was the only woman he would ever love. The only woman he would ever want to make a life with. And she'd believed him.

Saddened by the precious memories, Victoria rose to her feet. "I'm hardly a femme fatale, Jess. And I can see my coming here was a mistake."

She took one step toward the door before he was instantly on his feet, blocking her exit. "Why?" he asked, his voice quietly demanding. "Does seeing me again bother you that much?"

Yes, she wanted to scream. Everything about him, from his musky male scent to his rugged features, made her ache with bitter loss.

Her gaze lifted to scan his face. "This conversation is pointless."

A tiny grin tugged at the corners of his lips. "I don't know about that," he drawled. "I'm learning lots of things from this meeting."

Feeling more than exposed, she folded her arms against her breasts. "Like what?"

Amusement deepened the lines bracketing his mouth. "Like you're not nearly as indifferent to me as you want to believe."

The air whooshed from her lungs. "Dream on."

One step brought him so close that the front of his starched shirt was almost brushing the tips of her breasts. Inside, Victoria trembled like a little lost dogie in a snowdrift.

"I don't have to dream," he countered arrogantly. "I kissed you the other day, remember? You didn't exactly resist."

Her face flamed as heat rushed from the soles of her feet all the way to her scalp. "That was a purely physical reaction!"

His brows lifted mockingly. "You analyze all your kisses that way, Doc?"

She didn't have any kisses to analyze. But she wasn't about to admit such a thing to him. She didn't want him to learn that after him, she'd forsaken men. She wouldn't give him the satisfaction of knowing he'd ruined any chances of her loving another man.

"I didn't come here to discuss kisses!" she said, her voice rising with each word. "I came here to see if you'd made any progress on finding out the identity of the body!"

Unaffected by her outburst, he said in a voice that could only be described as a purr, "If you ask me, I think the kissing is much more interesting."

Her teeth ground together as her gaze whipped over his leering face. "Why? I'm sure a man like you has all sorts of women to discuss such frivolous things with."

His features twisted with even more sarcasm. "Yeah, but me and my...women don't have a past like you and I do."

To her horror, tears were suddenly collecting in her

throat, sending a fiery ball of pain to the middle of her chest. "Our past—is forgotten," she said tightly.

The taunting expression on his face suddenly disappeared and before she realized his intentions, his hands were on her shoulders, their warmth radiating up the sides of her neck and down her arms.

"Not for me, Tori."

"Why?" she whispered huskily. "There can be no good in us remembering."

His fingers tightened perceptively. "Something happens to a man when he's rejected by the woman he loves. It flattens his self-worth. It makes him keep wondering why."

Victoria couldn't continue to look at him. It hurt too much. Instead, she turned her back to him and drew in a ragged breath that seared her lungs. "We both know you never loved me, Jess. So don't try to act like the injured soul."

A tense, pregnant moment passed. Finally he said in a soft, accusing voice, "You don't know anything about me. I don't believe you ever did."

She swallowed, struggling to push down the tears that continued to scald her throat. "I know enough. I know that if you'd really wanted me, you wouldn't have let me go. You wouldn't have walked away. And you wouldn't have waited four years to come back."

Behind her, Jess closed his eyes while silently cursing himself. He shouldn't be saying any of this to her. She was right. All that had happened between them was over. Long in the past. Yet in his heart their affair was as fresh as the scent of flowers on her skin.

"Maybe I was waiting on you to come to me," he countered.

Gasping softly, she whirled to face him. "That's a lie. If I heard correctly, you got married not long after you went to El Paso."

Shadows flickered in his gray eyes as he tried to tamp down a barrage of bitter emotions. "After a few months I had to accept you weren't ever going to change. Or leave your daddy. I had to get on with my life."

Back then, the news of Jess's marriage had very nearly destroyed Victoria. Even now the idea crushed her with loss and regret. She'd desperately wanted to marry him, be his wife and make their home on the Hastings ranch. But then he'd gotten the chance to join the border patrol and suddenly it was more important for him to go to Texas than to stay in New Mexico with her.

Looking back on it now, Victoria could see he'd been testing her, forcing her to choose between going with him or staying behind with her father. No woman should be forced to make such a choice, she thought sadly. Either option was going to make her a loser. And it had. She'd not only lost Jess, but now her father was gone from her life, too.

"Is that why you haven't spoken to me since you've come back to San Juan County?" she asked him. "Because your wife would be jealous? Or did you ever tell her about me?"

He stared at her, his brow puckered with a bewildered frown. "Don't tell me you haven't heard?"

Victoria shook her head as a strange premonition washed over her. "Heard what? That you're divorced? That doesn't surprise me. You certainly aren't behaving as if you're a married man."

The frown on his face deepened and she watched him swallow convulsively as he glanced away from her. "My wife and I divorced more than a year ago. But since then Regina was killed."

Stunned, Victoria stared at him. Why hadn't Alice or Will told her, she wondered. Had he ordered them not to? "I—I'm sorry. I didn't know," she murmured brokenly. "How? When?"

He turned his gaze back to her and Victoria decided his features looked as though they were carved from stone. "Seven months ago. In a car accident. She had our daughter with her at the time. But thank God Katrina wasn't even scratched."

His daughter! Jess had a child?

The room around her tilted as shock drained every ounce of color from her face. In a drawn voice, she asked, "You...have a daughter?"

He nodded and, for the first time since she'd seen him again, there was a real smile on his face.

"Yes, I have a daughter. Her name is Katrina," he answered. "She just turned two-and-a-half."

Victoria's gaze fell to the floor as painful emotions slammed at her from all directions. Of course it was a logical thing for him to have a child. He'd been a married man. But in her heart Jess wasn't supposed to have a daughter or son! Not without her.

"Congratulations," she said quietly, then glancing back up at him she tried to smile, but she could feel her lips quivering from the effort. Hopefully, he wouldn't notice her jerky smile or the dull pain in her eyes. "You must be very proud."

Jess stepped behind the desk and picked up a small, wooden framed photograph. "She was a few months

younger here," he said, handing the photo to Victoria.
"She's grown quite a bit since then."

Victoria studied the little round face topped with a
thick thatch of golden-red curls. Baby teeth gleamed
behind her impish grin. She resembled Jess in coloring
and the shape of her features.

Staring down at the baby girl's image, Victoria
could only wonder how a child of his and hers would
have looked. Like this one? Or would it have taken
after her with the Ketchum's dark hair and blue-green
eyes? *Don't think about it,* she scolded herself. *Jess
made his choice and it wasn't making a life with you.*

She handed the photo back to him. "She's very
beautiful, Jess."

With a humble smile, he nodded. "Katrina wasn't
planned. But she's definitely a blessing."

Victoria watched him place the photo back on his
desktop. "It must be…very hard trying to raise a little
girl without a mother."

"Ma helps. And the women who run the small day
care over by Cedar Hill are very good with her. I
realize it's not the same, but—" Once again he came
back around the desk to stand in front of her. "Regina
never was much of a mother to Katrina anyway. After
our divorce I was awarded custody."

Questions buzzed in Victoria's head, but she didn't
voice them. To ask any more about his personal life
these past four years would be admitting that she was
still interested. And she wasn't! She couldn't be. Not
and keep her senses intact.

"And that's the way you wanted it? To have total
custody?"

He looked puzzled and more than a little offended

at her question. "I understand you think of me as a—
something lower than pond scum, but I do love my
daughter, Victoria. I don't want anyone raising her but
me."

Frustrated that he'd misunderstood, Victoria shook
her head. "I didn't mean—some men love their children very much but find they can't cope with raising
them alone. Especially babies. I'm honestly glad it's
different for you."

Deciding she couldn't take any more talk about
Jess's child, she started toward the door, "Now if
you'll excuse me, I'll let you get back to work."

Once again Jess was quick to block her path. Tilting
her head back, she looked up at him and was instantly
caught off guard by the intimate questions swirling in
his gray eyes.

"Why did you come here today, Tori?" he asked
softly. "Really?"

Her mouth fell open, then closed as the sound of
his voice, the nearness of his body, pulled on her like
a sensual rope. It didn't make sense that she could
still want this man, she told herself frantically. He was
a heartache just waiting to happen all over again.

"I told you," she answered. "To talk to Deputy
Redwing."

Mockery twisted his rugged features. "This is the
sheriff's department. My office is here. You didn't
think there was a chance of running into me?"

Lifting her chin, she said, "I knew there was a
chance. But you're not the plague. Even if I do happen
to cross your path, I'm not going to catch anything
deadly. And anyway, I'm a doctor. I can cure most
common afflictions."

He suddenly chuckled and the warm sound whirled her back to happier times. Back when all Jess had seemed to want was to have her in his arms.

"I'll remember that. Just in case I come down with one," he taunted, then almost instantly his expression turned serious. "As for your earlier questions, I don't have any news on the corpse. It was taken to a state forensics lab in Albuquerque for further investigation."

She was surprised and grateful that he'd decided to at least tell her this much about the case. "How long do you expect that to take?"

He shrugged. "There's no way of knowing. It depends on how busy they are down there. And, of course, on the types of tests run. Which, considering the condition of the remains, will probably be several. So I wouldn't plan on hearing anything for a while."

She nodded. "Being a doctor, I know how slowgoing some tests can be," she said, then with a sigh, she added, "In the meantime, I can only hope my patients will get all this gossiping out of their system."

"What are they saying?"

Victoria let out a long sigh. "Nothing in particular. Most of them are asking questions rather than expressing an opinion on the matter. But I will say all of them seem to have faith in you and Sheriff Perez."

Humor glinted in his eyes. "That's good to know."

She regarded him closely as she was struck with more questions. "There hasn't been anyone able to give you any sort of information or clues? What about missing persons? Did you check with Farmington? Bloomfield? Dulce?"

"Nothing from missing persons fits this case," he said, then seeing the worry on her face, he asked, "Why are you so concerned about this thing, Victoria? Is there something you haven't told me?"

Frowning, she stepped around him and this time managed to make it to the door before he could stop her. "I've already told you my worries," she said. "Anything else you'll have to figure out on your own."

"I plan to."

The subtle warning in his voice caused her to pause. She glanced back at him and her heart seemed to wince at the distant look on his face. "What does that mean?" she asked.

"Just what I said. I'm still in the process of questioning the wranglers and cowhands on the T Bar K."

Frowning, she said, "I thought you'd already done that."

He sauntered toward her and the unbidden thought struck Victoria that the years he'd been away had hardened him even more. Maybe losing his wife had done that to him, she thought sadly. Heaven knows he must have loved her. A man like Jess didn't have to marry a woman just to have her.

"The T Bar K is a big ranch," Jess reasoned. "You Ketchums employ a lot of men. Questioning all of them would take several days, even with Redwing's help."

Her fingers curled into loosely formed fists. "You're not going to let this thing go, are you? You're going to keep digging until you find something to pin on my family or one of our hands."

His expression turned to a look of disbelief. "That's not my intention, Victoria. I'm not—"

"Then why don't you write the whole thing off as an accident? We both know that's more than likely what happened. Some transient came along and fell to his death."

Insulted by her suggestion, he stepped closer, his nostrils flaring as his gray eyes slipped over her flushed face. "I'm not like your old man, Victoria. I don't make up facts beforehand or try to shade the truth once they're out."

She wasn't going to argue with him about her father. It would be pointless. Most everyone knew Jess hated Tucker. For his wealth and his bulldozing ways of acquiring it, not to mention the gossip of his extra-marital affairs. But mostly Jess hated Tucker because the old rancher hadn't wanted Victoria marrying a common man. And back then Jess had seen himself as common. She wondered if he still did.

As for Tucker, Victoria had always admitted he was far from perfect. But he'd been a loving father to her. Even now with the old man in his grave, she couldn't forget that.

"I'm not asking you to shade the truth!"

Jess shot her a wry smile. "I don't have the truth—yet, Victoria. That's why neither Sheriff Perez or I will rule this case in any way...until it's solved."

"And you have a Ketchum behind bars?" she asked tightly.

"Now why would I want that?"

His expression was so stone smooth, it was impossible to tell if his question had been spoken with sarcasm or sincerity. She figured the first.

"You are heading up this investigation, aren't you?"

"That's right."

"Then you could influence the outcome."

One more step brought him close enough to touch her. Victoria forced herself to remain where she was as his fingertips traced a circle on her cheek.

"I won't play favorites to you Ketchums, Victoria. So don't ask."

Anger and pain twisted through her. "I wouldn't dream of asking you for anything, Jess. I did once, remember? It got me nothing then. It wouldn't now."

"Victoria—"

She didn't give him the chance to say more. Quickly, she jerked the door open and stepped out of the room and out of his sight.

Chapter Four

"Yip! Yip! Yo cattle! Get along and quit dragging your tails!"

As Will called to the seven head of heifers and steers, Jess slapped a stiff lariat against the leg of his leather chap. The popping sound helped to drive the small herd into a makeshift catch pen.

Not seeing much of man since back in the deep of winter, the snaky cattle were wild and reluctant to be cornered. But Will and Jess had set up the portable fencing in a dry wash with steep banks on both sides. Once they'd gotten the animals headed into the gulch they had nowhere to go but forward.

Dust spiraled up from the stirring hooves, clinging red and thick to Jess's face and black hat. His gray horse was wet with sweat, his head hung low from the long exertion of the day. Jess was feeling the weariness, too, and no doubt his grandfather was getting stiff from long hours in the saddle.

The two of them had been working since sunrise and had already worn out four mounts between them. But northern New Mexico was rough land; ranching this area wasn't suited for a weak-willed person or animal. The harsh winters could sometimes wipe out half a man's herd while the steep mountains and rocky arroyos on the Hastings ranch had crippled many a good horse from time to time. But it was home. And Jess was glad to be back. Even if it meant he was closer to Victoria Ketchum.

"That looks like the last of 'em, Pa," Jess said to his grandfather as he wired the fence panel shut against the nervous cattle.

From his seat in the saddle, Will cast a glance at the setting sun. "Yeah. And not any too soon. It's gonna be dark before we get back to the ranch."

"That won't matter," Jess assured the old man. "Pokie and Star know the way. The horses could find the ranch even if they were blindfolded."

"Hell," Will muttered as he lifted his Stetson and wiped a sleeve across his leathery face, "me and you could find the way even if *we* was blindfolded. I was thinking about your ma. She's gonna be worried and thinking we've fell into an arroyo like that dead fella on the T Bar K."

Jess swung himself back into the saddle. "I don't think Ma needs to be worrying that something like that will happen to us."

With the cattle safely penned and given access to feed and water, the men turned their mounts toward home while the extra horses automatically trailed behind them.

As they rode up and out of the dry wash, Will said, "You don't think that dead man just stumbled on a rock and fell, do you?"

For the past week and a half the T Bar K case had been going round and round in Jess's head. So far, without the coroner's report, there wasn't much to go on. Except instinct. And something about the whole thing had been giving Jess a very bad feeling. He didn't exactly know why. Except that the body had been discovered in an extremely remote area without any access roads.

A transient, as Victoria had suggested, likely wouldn't have wandered so far off the highway. Even the primitive dirt roads petered out long before the spot where the body had been discovered. Why would a man deliberately leave civilized roads and head into rough land on foot? It didn't make sense to Jess.

"I don't know, Pa. Not yet."

"It's plain you don't know, son. I'm askin' you what you think?"

Jess untied a yellow bandanna from around his neck and wiped the scarf over his sweaty face. It came away as red as the ground they were riding over. "Just between me and you, it looks pretty suspicious." He glanced at Will. "Why? What have you been thinking about the whole thing?"

Will grunted. "I guess I've been thinkin' about the Ketchums. They've had their share of troubles over the years. Just goes to show you money don't fix everything. I'll bet Ross would pay a mighty big heap right about now to get all this quieted down."

Jess shot his grandfather a speculative look. "You think Tucker's son could be involved somehow?"

"Hell, if Tucker was alive, folks around these parts would already be shouting murder," Will said with a shrug of his shoulders. "But the younger Ketchum—I ain't gonna say. I don't believe he's as unfeelin' as the old man. I just think he'd rather not have all this bad talk goin' on about the T Bar K. Can't be good for cattle or horse business."

According to Victoria, it wasn't good for her medical practice either, Jess thought. Since she'd come to his office nearly a week ago, he'd neither seen nor heard from her. Oddly enough, he'd missed her even more than usual. And he knew it had been a bad mistake to touch her, to kiss her again after all this time. It had only aroused all those memories he'd tried to bury.

"No. It can't be good for the Ketchums," Jess agreed. Then, with another thoughtful glance at his grandfather, he asked, "When exactly did Tucker die?"

Will rubbed his whiskered chin as the two men and four horses plodded along in the gloaming, through the blue sage and hunkering stands of twisted juniper.

"Probably more than a year now."

Jess processed his grandfather's information. "Do you know of anyone the old man was angry with around that time? Or before that time? Was there anyone in particular he was feuding with?"

Will chuckled. "I doubt there's ever been a time when Tucker Ketchum wasn't having it out with someone around these parts. But I can't think of anyone in particular—" Will gave his grandson a sidelong glance. "Jess, you're forgettin' the old man was feeble for several months before he died. Spent his days in a wheelchair with an oxygen tank. He couldn't have knocked anybody in the head."

Jess snorted. "Tucker was too smart to do any job himself. He would have hired it done," he said, then his voice softening, he asked, "Was the old man really disabled for so long?"

Will sighed. "Yeah. The old man had all that land and cattle and money, but those things couldn't cure his heart. Victoria is the one I feel sorry for, though. She stood by her papa 'til the end, doctoring him. She didn't have a chance to get her own practice goin' 'til after Tucker died. These past four years haven't been much of a life for her."

They hadn't been much for Jess, either. Not without Victoria by his side. Will knew as much. This was just a subtle reminder from his grandfather that Jess shouldn't have left New Mexico or Victoria behind.

"She chose it," Jess clipped, then nudging his spurs into the horse's sides, he picked up the pace, forcing Will to follow suit.

The moment the two men rode into the ranch yard, Alice ran out of the house, waving her arms to catch the men's attention. Seeing her, Jess didn't bother dismounting. Instead, he loped the horse to the yard fence.

"What's wrong? I told you if the department needed me to call my pager."

Alice shook her head and by then Jess could see his grandmother was frantic with worry.

"It's not your work," she said as Jess quickly slid

out of the saddle. "It's Katrina. She started running a fever this afternoon. I can't get it down."

Rather than waste time going around through the gate, Jess vaulted over the yard fence. "Why didn't you take her into Aztec to the doctor?"

"Because today is Saturday. The medical clinic is closed. And anyway, she wasn't that bad until this evening. I was about to take her into the hospital emergency room when I saw you two ride up."

"Where is she?" he asked, already on his way through the front door.

"In her crib," Alice answered as she trotted frantically to keep up with him. "What—are you going to do?"

Inside the baby's bedroom a lamp was on, shedding a pool of light over the sleeping child. Jess's heart clutched with fear as he took in his daughter's little red face and hot, dry skin.

"I don't want to take her to the hospital. All of the machines and strange faces would scare her."

"But Jess, she needs medical attention! I—"

Before his grandmother could finish, Jess was stuffing diapers and extra clothing into a diaper bag. At this moment nothing mattered but his daughter.

"I am going to get her medical attention, Ma. I'm taking her over to the T Bar K. To Victoria."

Chapter Five

Nearly a half hour later, Jess braked his truck to a stop in front of the Ketchum ranch house. The porch was illuminated with light and, as he killed the motor and reached for Katrina, he could see Victoria stepping through the door.

On his drive over, he'd called on his cell phone to make sure Victoria would be home. Jess hadn't talked to her, but Marina had assured him she would give her the message. Apparently the cook had come through with her promise.

By the time he stood down on the ground with the baby in his arms, Victoria was standing outside the door of the truck. When he looked at her face, the only thing he saw was concern.

"Did she hurt herself or is she ill?" Victoria quickly asked as she stepped toward father and daughter. "Marina sometimes has trouble with her English. She wasn't exactly sure what you'd told her over the phone."

"She's burning up with fever," Jess told her.

Victoria didn't waste time pulling back the blanket Jess had swaddled around the child. Instead, she motioned for him to follow her into the house.

"There's a room in the back of the house I use for an infirmary for the ranch. I'll examine her there," she told Jess.

Victoria hurried across a large living room, then down a hallway through the left wing of the house. At the last door, she pushed it open and gestured for Jess to precede her.

Overhead florescent lighting illuminated a small room equipped with an examining table, several cabinets with glass doors, a wooden desk, a sink, refrigerator, a single bed and straight-backed chair.

"She's so hot it feels like I'm carrying a sack of coals," Jess said as he glanced around him. "Where do you want her? On the examining table?"

"Please," Victoria answered while pushing back the sleeves of her sweater. Reaching for a stethoscope, she asked, "How long has she had a fever?"

"I'm not sure. The way Ma talked she's had a temperature off and on all day. It wasn't until this evening that she couldn't get it to go down."

Stepping forward, Victoria quickly stripped away the blanket covering the child, then pulled the thin T-shirt she was wearing gently over her head. After placing a thermometer under the baby's arm, she ran her fingers over Katrina's red cheek, then inspected the rosy rash on her chest and stomach.

''All the way over here, she didn't whimper or say a word,'' Jess spoke hoarsely. ''I tried to wake her once. She just looked at me with glazed sort of eyes.''

''That's not unusual with fever this high,'' Victoria told him as she continued to carefully examine the little girl. ''Has your daughter been sick recently?''

Jess remained by Victoria's side, watching as she placed the stethoscope to his baby's chest. Fear knotted his throat, making him wonder if he could manage to speak at all.

''No. Other than a cold once in a while, she's always been very healthy.''

Victoria nodded with approval. Jess's daughter appeared to be a little above average size for her age and her muscles were physically fit. Sure signs she received plenty of healthy food and exercise.

''Has she been coughing? Sneezing?''

''Not that I've noticed.''

Victoria looked in both ears, then depressed the child's tongue to inspect her throat. ''Oh my. This is a mess. Has she been in a public place recently?''

''Ma takes her to the grocery store and places like that.''

''What about a medical facility?'' Victoria asked as she read the thermometer.

Jess pulled off his hat and raked a hand through his hair. ''I—uh—don't know. I haven't—'' He stopped suddenly as a thought struck him. ''Wait, I think Ma took Katrina to the health clinic a few days ago for some sort of immunization.'' He shot Victoria a frantic look. ''Why? Is this some sort of reaction to the shots?''

Victoria quickly shook her head to dispel the question. "No. But it could be a result of her being there in the building."

Jess's gaze flew to Katrina, who was lying so deathly still it terrified him. Even though his marriage had been a disaster, his daughter was very precious to him. He loved her more than his whole life.

"What's wrong with her? You said her throat was a mess. Is it strep throat?"

"No. But she's been infected with the same sort of bacteria that causes strep. I'm fairly certain your daughter has scarlet fever. The rash on her skin is a telltale sign, along with the fever."

Staggered by the news, Jess stared at her. "Scarlet fever! What is that? What does it mean? Will she—"

Victoria held up her hand to slow his racing questions. "First of all, Jess, calm down. Your daughter is going to be all right."

Slowly, a heavy breath pushed past his lips and then his gaze waffled from Katrina to Victoria. "Are you sure?"

His uncertainty of her judgment caused Victoria's eyes to fill with disappointment. "I like to think you brought Katrina here tonight because you trust me as a doctor."

Jess grimaced. As a doctor he knew she was highly intelligent, dedicated and without fault. It was the woman in her he couldn't trust. But he wasn't here tonight because he'd once loved this woman, he told himself. She was a capable doctor and at the moment that was all that mattered.

"I do trust you," he said quietly.

"Good. Then believe me when I tell you Katrina

will be fine once she's given the right care. Now, can you tell me if she can take penicillin?''

Jess nodded. "She's not allergic. She's taken it before.''

Victoria quickly crossed the small room and pulled a vial from the refrigerator. "That's very good news. I'll get her started on medication right now.'' She pulled a packaged syringe from a nearby drawer. "Scarlet fever is a communicable disease,'' she went on. "I haven't seen it in my office in a long time. But some cases could have passed through the public health clinic recently. Katrina picked up the bacteria from some other infected child.''

Standing beside his daughter, Jess's expression turned to one of anguish as he watched Victoria fill the syringe.

"She has to have a shot? Can't you give her oral medication?''

That Jess loved his daughter didn't surprise Victoria. But his showing it did. He'd always been a tough man. A man's man, who kept the tender side of his emotions hidden. Being a father had changed him to some degree, she supposed. But obviously not nearly enough to make him forgive and forget their past.

Emotion knotted her throat, forcing her to clear it before she could answer. "I'm afraid not, Jess. The disease is too far progressed. You might as well get used to the idea of her being pricked with a needle because she's going to require injections for the next few days.''

"Will she have to be hospitalized? She's so little. I don't want her to be scared. If there's any—''

Returning to the examining table, Victoria shook

her head. "She doesn't have to go to the hospital, Jess. We can treat her at home." She inclined her head toward the listless child. "Would you turn her onto her side? And you might want to hold her while I'm doing this. Just in case the sting of the needle rouses her."

Jess gently maneuvered Katrina so that her hip was exposed. He watched Victoria quickly swab a spot with antiseptic, then after that he had to look away.

"I notice your daughter is wearing training pants, not a diaper," Victoria mused aloud. "Is she already potty trained?"

"Yes. And she rarely has an accident. But with her being sick like this I can't promise she won't."

A strange lump of pain gathered in Victoria's chest as she watched Jess's big hand swipe at the golden red curls on the baby's forehead. For a long time she'd dreamed of having a child of her own—with Jess. She supposed that doctoring Katrina was as close to her dream as she would ever get.

"I wasn't worried about her having an accident," Victoria told him. "I was just thinking she's very young to already be out of diapers. She must be a smart little girl."

"She is. Smart enough to know she doesn't like her clothes wet."

Victoria found it hard to imagine this man changing diapers, much less potty-training a toddler. He'd always been an outdoorsman. His big hands were made for handling horses, roping and branding cattle, shooting a rifle or revolver. And loving a woman. She'd not ever pictured him dressing a baby girl in ruffles and lace. But then she'd never expected him to be the father of a motherless child.

"The penicillin will start to work now." She pulled the needle from the baby's hip and tossed it into a nearby disposal. "In the meantime, I'll sponge her down with cool water and see if that will lower her temperature a bit."

When he didn't respond, she looked up at him, and for the first time this evening, she allowed herself to take in his nearness and to wonder why he'd brought his daughter to her rather than rushing her to the emergency room in Aztec. She wanted to think it was because he still cared for her, that he trusted her with the life of his child. But with Jess it was difficult to read his motives.

Reaching over Katrina, she touched his forearm. "Don't worry," she gently placated, "Katrina is going to get well."

The knot of anxiety in Jess's stomach eased somewhat, but it didn't go away entirely. It wouldn't go away until he saw his daughter laughing and playing. "How long will it take for her to get over this scarlet fever? What kind of care will she need?"

Victoria thought for only a second before she answered. "You don't need to worry about that, either, Jess. I'll take care of Katrina for the next few days."

Jess's mind had been so fuzzed with worry for the past hour it took him several moments to realize exactly what Victoria meant.

"You?" he asked incredulously. "You can't take care of my daughter!"

His outburst brought a wry smile to Victoria's face.

"If an M.D. isn't qualified to care for her, then I don't know who would be."

Still skeptical, he stared at her. "That's not what I mean. I know you can treat her, but—"

She crossed the room to gather water and a wash-cloth. "But what?" she asked, her back to him as she filled a plastic basin.

His eyes slid down the length of her. She was wearing a mint-green skirt and matching sweater. Both cleaved to her curves just enough to be tempting. Her dark hair was loose against her back, the front kept away from her face with a twisted scarf. She was a woman with everything. Beauty, brains and money. She was also a Ketchum. And he'd once made the mistake of thinking that didn't matter. He wouldn't make the same mistake again.

"I can take care of my own child, Victoria."

She closed her eyes for a moment and reminded herself she was a doctor in need, not a woman scorned. "You have a job that can call you away at any given moment."

"Ma will be there to help with Katrina."

She looked over her shoulder at him. "Your grandmother isn't a young woman. She already has plenty of work to do around the ranch without the added stress of caring for a sick baby."

Victoria was right, of course. But that didn't mean she should take care of his kid, Jess reasoned with himself. "If I'm lucky I won't be called out on an emergency. Besides, you have your own medical clinic to run. You can't stay home just to take care of my daughter," he argued.

Carrying the basin of water, she crossed the small

space to him and the baby. "Would you please put her on the bed where she'll be more comfortable," she instructed, then added, "You might feel like arguing about the matter, Jess, but this little girl needs relief from whomever she can get it."

His features tight, Jess lifted Katrina over to the single bed. Victoria quickly eased down beside her and after wringing out the wet cloth began to wipe it over the child's red face and chest.

"Do you know the last time she was given a fever reducer?" Victoria asked, acutely aware that Jess was watching her every move.

"No."

"Would you mind calling your grandmother to find out? I don't want to overdose her. There's a phone over there in the corner. On the desk."

Jess went to the instrument and punched in the number. Alice was relieved to hear from him and after a brief explanation as to what was going on, he hung up and rejoined Victoria, who continued to sponge Katrina with the cool water.

"She said she gave Katrina a dose of acetaminophen at four this evening," Jess told her.

Victoria glanced at her wristwatch. It was only seven. Dear Lord it seemed like midnight. But Jess had a way of draining her energy. Even so, his child was in desperate need of medical care and Victoria's heart had already made a decision to give it to her. In spite of her disturbing reaction to Jess's presence.

"I'll give her something in an hour," she said for his benefit. "In the meantime, this should help cool down her body temperature."

Uncertainty swamped him. "Maybe I should take her to the hospital."

"I've already done what a doctor there would do for her, Jess. And you're right, it's traumatic for a child this young to be in a strange environment like a hospital." Her mind set, she glanced up at him. "I have a friend who's a retired doctor. He sits in for me when I need time away from the office. He'll be glad to take over while I care for Katrina. He misses his work."

Jess let out a heavy breath. "Why are you making this so easy for me?"

Victoria's gaze fell back to the baby. "You came to me for help. That's all I'm trying to do, Jess. Help you."

Maybe so. But why, he asked himself. His daughter was no different than any other patient that came through her office. He told himself he should feel honored, grateful, that she was willing to do so much for Katrina and forget about what, if any, motives she had.

"I didn't expect this much from you, Victoria. And I'm fairly certain you don't normally bring patients home with you."

She was going above and beyond the call of duty where this child was concerned, Victoria silently admitted. And she wasn't even sure why. Except that the moment she'd glanced down at the little girl and saw the resemblance of Jess in her tiny features, her heart had been stolen.

"That's true. But like I told you, scarlet fever is infectious. There's no need to take her elsewhere and spread the germs even more. And if you're thinking—'' She paused as her expression suddenly turned rueful.

''Thinking what?'' Jess urged.

Victoria squeezed the excess water from the cloth, then carefully draped it over Katrina's chest.

Her eyes on the child, she said, ''That I'm doing this for future favors. If you are, then I'll remind you that I'm not stupid.''

He scowled as he mulled over her words. ''Future favors. What do you mean?''

She looked up at him, her gaze unwavering. ''You're the undersheriff. You could pull legal strings.''

For a moment her comment stunned him. He'd not been thinking in that direction at all. It disgusted him because he hadn't. Because he'd been fool enough to think her compassion toward Katrina might have something to do with the closeness the two of them had once shared.

''I don't pull strings for anyone,'' he said gruffly. ''And that includes myself.''

His stony features cut her even more than his words. ''You don't have to tell me that, Jess. I know the sort of man you are.''

Did she really, Jess asked himself. He didn't think so. She hadn't understood him four years ago when he'd loved her so much he'd wanted to give her the world. She hadn't understood it was important for him to step up the ladder, to be admired and respected by his peers and the folks of the county, not just for himself, but for her sake, too. If he'd given in to her wishes and become a hired hand for her daddy, he would have wound up being Mr. Ketchum rather than Victoria being Mrs. Hastings.

"That's why it should be plain to you," she went on before he could make any sort of reply, "that I'm not taking care of your daughter for any sort of favors. I simply want to do it. For her. And you."

He stepped closer as warring emotions tugged him from one side of the fence to the other. "I can believe you would want to help a child. Any child. But not me. So let's leave *me* out of it."

Victoria told herself she was an idiot for letting his comments hurt her. After all this time and all these years of nothing from him, she ought to understand that Jess didn't even like her, much less harbor any sort of tender feelings toward her. But she was a sucker for children. And Katrina being his child just made her all the more special.

She blew out a heavy breath. "Now isn't the time for this, Jess. Getting Katrina well is all that matters. Don't you agree?"

Long moments passed without a response from him. Victoria finally glanced up to see him wiping a hand over his haggard face.

"You're right," he agreed in a low voice. "I came here for your help. I should be thanking you. Not questioning your motives."

His admission not only surprised her, it also touched a soft spot deep inside her. Shaken, she did her best to hide it by smiling and making light of the moment.

"You're a lawman, Jess. Questioning people's motives comes naturally to you." Desperate to get off the subject, she lifted the basin up to him. "Now if you'd like to help, you could pour this out and fill it with fresh water.''

Glad to do something other than stand helplessly by, he took the plastic basin and carried it over to the sink.

"You were saying Katrina's fever is contagious,'' Jess said. "I don't want her being here to cause a problem for your brother or anyone else on the ranch.''

"Scarlet fever is mostly a child's disease. And anyway, Ross is going to be out of the state for the next week or two. Marina and I will be the only ones staying here in the ranch house. Having Katrina here won't cause any problems,'' she reassured him.

He carried the water back to Victoria. "Then I guess it's settled. She stays with you,'' he said, his gaze dropping to his daughter's flushed face.

It suddenly dawned on Victoria that it wasn't having Katrina staying on the T Bar K that was bothering him. It was the idea of leaving her.

"Jess, you didn't imagine I expected you to have to leave, did you?''

His eyes suddenly darted to Victoria and he stared at her with disbelief. "I sure as hell didn't plan to stay here!''

"Why?'' she asked quietly.

His upper lip curled with mockery. "Do you have to ask?''

Ignoring his pointed suggestion, she replaced the thermometer under Katrina's arm. "I am a qualified physician,'' she stated firmly. "I can take care of your daughter's medical needs. But you are her father. She's going to need you, too. Especially when her fever starts to drop and she becomes aware of her surroundings. I expect she's close to you?''

Victoria's question brought a faint smile to Jess's face. Katrina had always been a daddy's girl. As soon as his daughter had become mobile, she'd followed him from room to room and yelled loudly if he went outside without her.

''You could say that. It's only been this past month that she doesn't scream when I leave for work.''

Victoria smiled with understanding. ''Then I have a feeling you'd better be around here or she's going to do a lot more screaming.''

Victoria was right. He couldn't just leave his daughter here without any of her family to make her feel safe and anchored. He needed to be here for Katrina. At least, as much as his job would allow. But staying under the same roof with Victoria? And on Ketchum land? Both were unsettling thoughts. Other than his visit here as the undersheriff, Jess hadn't been on the T Bar K in probably five years.

When he and Victoria had first started dating, he'd tried to be sociable with her family. And on the surface, Tucker had welcomed him into their home. But Jess hadn't been fooled. He'd felt hard resentment running beneath the old man's outward friendliness. He'd seen the disdain in Tucker's eyes when he thought Jess hadn't been looking.

The whole situation had been humiliating for Jess and eventually he'd refused to submit himself to Tucker's subterfuge, and had stayed away from the ranch entirely. Victoria had never understood why. But the old man was gone now, Jess reminded himself. And he'd do whatever it took to make his daughter well again.

"What is your brother going to say about me being here?" Jess asked. "He might not like it."

Victoria waved her hand dismissively. "Ross has enough problems of his own to deal with right now. And anyway, he never held any ill will toward you. He simply regards you as...my old flame. Nothing more."

Old flame. The two words mocked Jess. Each time he thought of Victoria or looked at her, the heat of desire flared up in him like a blowtorch. For him, the fire had never died. In spite of all his efforts to douse it.

Jess grunted sardonically. "Hmmph. I don't know whether to be insulted or grateful. Maybe I should just be thankful Tucker isn't still around or he would have already thrown me off the place. My daughter, too, probably."

Victoria glared at him. "My father loved children. He wouldn't have done something so heartless. But I guess it makes you feel good to paint him a monster."

Slightly ashamed of himself, Jess quickly shook his head. "Forget I said that, Victoria. It was out of line. I guess...having Katrina sick like this is making me say things I wouldn't ordinarily say. I shouldn't be lashing out at you. You're only trying to help."

"You've already said that once. And I know you're worried. You don't have to say it again."

His gaze focused on a spot between the toes of his boots, Jess jammed his hands in the pockets of his jeans, then realized as he did that he was still in his work clothes. Dust covered him from head to toe while cow manure had dried in splotches on his jeans and was caked on the soles of his boots. Once his grandmother had met him at the fence to tell him about Katrina, he'd not taken the time to even take off his spurs much less change clothes.

"I have a diaper bag in the truck with a few of Katrina's clothes. But if I'm going to stay here tonight, I'd better go back to the ranch and get a few things. I smell like a feedlot," he said after a moment.

"There's no need for you to make that long drive tonight. I can find something of Ross's for you to change into." She checked the thermometer once again. "Good. It's dropped a couple of degrees."

Victoria rose to her feet. "Stay here with her. I'll be back in a few minutes."

A short time passed before Victoria returned to the room. This time Marina was with her. The cook inclined her head toward Jess before turning her attention to Katrina.

"I'll keep watch," she promised Victoria, then took a seat on the edge of the bed beside the little girl. Her large, work worn hand gently soothed over Katrina's fevered brow. "You go take care of things. Nothin' will happen to this little *chica* while Marina is here."

Victoria motioned for Jess to follow her out of the room. Once they were in the hallway, she said, "Marina will watch her closely, let me know if there's any changes. Right now, I'll show you where you'll be sleeping tonight."

He was more than grateful for the care the two women were giving his daughter, but he still felt awkward and out of place in this house that, in size alone, would equal four or five of his grandparents' home.

Coupled with his passionate history with Victoria, he doubted he'd ever be able to relax as long as he was under this Ketchum roof.

"I don't need a room or anything. I doubt I'll be doing any sleeping anyway. Not until Katrina gets better."

Dismissing his comment as foolish, she started down the hallway, forcing Jess to follow.

"Don't be silly. You can't sit in a chair all night. That isn't going to do your daughter any good. Besides, I expect her to continue sleeping through this worst part. Tonight the medicine will begin to work. Tomorrow she'll start rousing around."

Jess didn't question her prediction. After all, she was the doctor. And like he'd told her earlier, he trusted her ability as a physician. What he needed to do the most was forget she'd once been his lover.

After passing several openings to other rooms, she entered a doorway to her left. A lamp was burning at the head of a four-poster bed, illuminating the intricate patchwork quilt covering the mattress. At the foot, a neat stack of clothes was ready and waiting for him.

Glancing quickly around him, Jess noticed the walls were varnished pine, the ceiling low and supported by huge beams. Along with the bed and nightstand, there was also a chest, dresser and stuffed armchair. On the west wall, a paned window ran from ceiling to floor, but darkness shrouded the view. From the lay of the house, Jess figured daylight would reveal a rocky pine bluff.

"I hope this isn't Ross's room," he said, a little amazed that she was setting him up so nicely.

"No. It's a guest room. Ross stays in the opposite wing of the house."

Pausing at the foot of the bed, he turned slightly as she came up behind him. "And where do you stay?" he asked, his gray eyes connecting with her dark green gaze.

Victoria swallowed as memories, hot and wild and delicious, skittered through her brain like the slow-motion frames of a movie camera. "I'll be across the hall from you."

So that meant even if Ross was home, the two of them would be more or less secluded. How the hell was he going to keep that out of his mind, he wondered.

"And I'll have Katrina with me," she went on, making Jess wonder if she could read his thoughts.

"Fine," he said, then raking a hand through his hair, he turned his attention to the stack of clothes. Just glancing, he could see blue jeans, cotton chambray shirts and white boxer shorts. "If you'll show me where I can shower, I'll get out of these nasty things. I don't imagine Marina appreciates cow manure being left all over her clean floors."

"She won't think anything of the manure. Ross and the hands are always tracking up the place." She moved closer, her hands circling the fat bedpost as she regarded him thoughtfully. "I take it from your dirty clothes that you weren't on duty today?"

"No. I've been helping Pa with roundup for the past couple of days. We aren't finished, but close enough that he can handle the rest."

A soft smile briefly touched her face. "How is your grandfather? I haven't seen him in a while."

Did she ever see Will or his grandmother, Jess wondered. If she did, his grandparents didn't mention it. But then they wouldn't. Not if they thought it would upset him.

"He can still sit a horse as well as me or any other man."

She nodded with approval. "That's good to hear. And your grandmother?"

"She hasn't slowed down much either."

"You're lucky to have them. And your daughter," she added, her voice dropping to a husky level. "She has to be a blessing."

He shot her a sidelong glance and was immediately surprised at how much the shadows on her face got to him. Her mother had been dead for nearly five years now, her father for more than a year. And if Jess remembered correctly, both sets of her grandparents had passed on when Victoria had been a small child. Other than her brothers, Ross and Seth, she had no family now.

Jess had never wished such loss on Victoria. In truth, if it had been left up to him, he would have seen that the two of them had made their own family, together. But she'd not chosen that path. She'd chosen to make her life without him. And the fact was still like a knife twisting in his gut.

"Yeah. I'm fortunate to have them."

Hearing the hardened edge to his voice, Victoria decided it was time to move away from the subject of family and get back to the matter at hand.

Stepping around him, she walked over to one corner of the room and opened a door that was made of the same pine planks as the wall.

"Here's the bathroom," she said, her back to him as she made a visual inspection of the small facilities. "I've left you towels, disposable razors, shaving cream and a few other toiletries I thought you might need. If you need anything else, just let me or Marina know."

Jess walked up behind her and immediately felt himself quiver inside as he breathed in her sweet, feminine scent. "I won't need anything else." *Except you, Victoria.* The unbidden thought brought him up short and tightened his features with self-disgust. He didn't know why, after all the years and all the pain that had separated them, he could still want her. But he did. And he hated himself for the weakness.

The nearness of his voice set Victoria's heart to pounding. Slowly she turned to find him only a step away. He smelled of horses and cattle, dust and sweat and sagebrush. A scent that reminded her Jess was all man. A man she'd wanted like no other. The thought momentarily paralyzed her lungs as she tilted her head back and studied his face.

"I'm glad you brought Katrina to me tonight," she said with open honesty.

Her finely honed features were softly lit by the muted glow of the lamp and his nostrils flared ever so slightly as his gaze slowly scanned their incredible beauty. "I suppose I should thank you again. I—"

The pent-up air whooshed from her lungs and without thinking, she stepped forward and touched her fingers to his lips. "Don't keep thanking me, Jess. That's not what I want from you. I never want you to feel beholden to me. For anything."

Surprise, then something savage flickered and darkened the depth of his eyes. Slowly his fingers curled around her slender forearms, and then so quickly she didn't know what had happened, he had her arms behind her back and her breasts were crushed against his dusty shirt.

"I'd like to know just what it is you want from me, Victoria," he said gruffly. "Is it sex? Are you too proud to ask some of your rich male friends for a night in the sack? Is it easier with me because I come from rough stock?"

Wide-eyed, she stared at him. "You're crazy!" she whispered accusingly.

One brow arched sardonically. "Maybe. Maybe not. But you're forgetting that I know you, Victoria. I've seen that hungry look on your face before."

She couldn't breathe or think. Nor could she stop the wild, rapid beat of her heart. "What look?" she asked, trying her best to sound both casual and ignorant.

His lips curved to form rueful creases along either side of his mouth. "The one on your face a few moments ago. The one where you were asking me to do this."

"This? I don't—"

Before she could get another word out, Jess had lowered his head and was murmuring against her lips. "Tell me you don't want me to kiss you. To make love to you."

She couldn't admit to something so untrue. And furthermore he knew it. "Jess—"

The whisper of his name snapped Jess back to reality and he thrust her from him as though she were a hot coal scorching him with fire.

Turning his back to her, he sucked in several ragged breaths while mentally cursing himself for his reckless behavior. This couldn't happen again. Even if she wanted it. Or he wanted it. He couldn't make the mistake of loving her again.

More moments passed and he realized Victoria was still standing behind him. Waiting. For what, he didn't know. Surely she didn't think he was going to change his mind about her. Or the two of them making love.

"Don't you think you should be leaving?" he finally asked.

Her face was expressionless. Except for her eyes, which seemed to be peering right to the core of his being.

"Is that what you really want?" she asked softly.

No. Damn it.

Aloud, he said, "The only reason I'm here is Katrina. And from now on, I promise you I won't forget that."

Her dark eyes continued to search his face and he could see she was trying to make sense of his words and behavior. After a while she must have realized he could give her no answers. She turned and left the room, leaving Jess to slump against the doorjamb and wait for the awful, aching need in him to ease.

Chapter Six

Jess had just dried off from a shower and was stepping into his jeans when someone knocked on the bedroom door. Quickly he dealt with the zipper, then shrugged into one of the chambray shirts.

Not bothering with the buttons, he slicked back his wet hair with one hand while opening the door with the other. The sight of Marina standing grim-faced on the other side instantly pricked him with concern.

"What's wrong?"

The longtime cook of the Ketchum family shook her head to reassure him that nothing had changed for the worse with his daughter. "Victoria says for me to feed you. Your meal is in the kitchen."

At one time, Marina had liked Jess. She'd gone out of her way to be friendly with him. But that was before Jess had left for Texas. Apparently she viewed his leaving as a man deserting the woman who loved him. The old woman probably didn't have any idea that Jess had practically begged Victoria to go with him, but that she'd chosen to remain here on the T Bar K and hold her daddy's hand.

"Thank you, Marina. I'll be there in a few minutes."

Nodding, she turned to leave, then glanced back at him, her expression sorrowful. "I'm sorry your little girl is sick. But Victoria will make her well again."

The cook's empathy surprised Jess and touched him more than he would have expected it to. For a long time he'd tried to tell himself that no one here on the T Bar K mattered to him, that they could all go to hell. But that had only been the scarred, angry part of him talking. Marina reminded him of his grandmother, who'd worked all her life for her family. The two women weren't highly educated, but they were both ambitious, loving and full of the wisdom of life. He couldn't help but respect and admire them.

"Thanks, Marina. And I believe you're right. I believe Victoria will make her well."

The woman's narrowed gaze keenly roamed his face. "Is that the only reason you are here on the T Bar K? To get your daughter well?"

Jess thought for only a moment before he answered, "Yes. That's the only reason."

The older woman's grim expression relaxed somewhat and her black eyes softened. "That's good. I wouldn't like for Victoria to be all hurt again."

By him? Or by the law, Jess wondered. But he didn't have the chance to ask. Already, Marina was walking away from him.

A few minutes later, in the kitchen, he'd just finished a bowl of stew and was starting on a piece of apple crumb pie when Victoria appeared in the room.

The sight of her made him immediately fear the worst. "Has her fever come back up?" he asked quickly.

Victoria came to stand beside the long pine table that filled up the center of the kitchen. It was scarred from years of use, but she preferred to take her meals on it rather than the expensive oak table in the dining room.

As small children, she and her brothers had spent many an hour here in the kitchen with their mother and Marina. Those precious memories always warmed Victoria. Too bad her memories of Jess weren't as easy to digest, she thought.

"No," she answered his question. "A few minutes ago I gave her another dose of fever reducer. And she managed to sip a bit of water."

"Thank God," he said quietly.

Victoria noticed he was dressed in her brother's clean clothes, his face shaved clean, his sandy hair still damp and curled ever so slightly against the back of his collar. Fatigue shadowed his eyes and she wondered why that should bother her. Or why just looking at the hard line of his lips made her ache. Back in his room, he'd made it plain he wanted nothing to do with her. She should be glad. Relieved. Yet she felt empty and full of regret.

"I see Marina fed you."

Nodding, he eased his stiff shoulders against the back of the chair. "She's still one of the best cooks in these parts."

Affection softened Victoria's expression. "I hope you told her that. She doesn't get enough praise for her work."

"I did," Jess said. "But I don't think it scored any points with her. She'll probably be glad to see the last of me."

Barely concealing a sigh, Victoria pulled out a chair and sat down facing him. "You think everyone looks down on you, don't you?"

"No. Just everyone on the T Bar K."

"Maybe that's just your guilty conscious rearing its head," she couldn't stop from saying.

His eyes narrowed as his fork sliced into the pie. "I don't have anything to feel guilty about."

A wan smile tilted her lips. "Then I guess you simply have a chip on your shoulder."

Jess could see she was goading him. To pick up where they'd left off in the bedroom, he suspected. But he wasn't going to play her game. Whatever that was. She was too tempting and he was a smart enough man to know she'd have him turned inside out if he gave her just the tiniest chance.

"Think that if it makes you happy, Victoria. But I won't argue with you tonight."

She'd not really wanted to argue with him or criticize him in any way. She simply wanted him to understand he'd not been hated or even disliked by anyone. Including her father. But that was all in the past, she thought wearily. She doubted anything could ever make Jess admit that their broken relationship had been partly his fault.

"I'm not in the mood for arguing either," she said, forcing a brighter note to her voice. "And anyway, I need your help. I called Maggie a few minutes ago and she still has Aaron's crib stored away in her garage. I need for you to haul it over here and set it up in my bedroom.''

She was going to a lot of trouble for his daughter and once again he wondered why. To be on his good side just in case the Ketchums were somehow connected to the unidentified body? Dear Lord, he couldn't let himself think such a thing right now. Maybe later he'd be forced to deal with such a problem. But at this moment all he wanted was for Katrina to be well. Afterwards…well, he'd be a lawman again.

''Of course I'll help you get the bed.'' He tossed down his napkin. ''Are you ready to go now?''

She inclined her head to his half-eaten pie. ''You finish that while I go tell Marina to keep an eye on Katrina until we get back.''

Hugh Ketchum's widow also lived on the T Bar K. The house, though modest in size and style compared to the main ranch house, would still be considered lavish by regular folks like Jess.

Being only a half mile away, the trip to Maggie's took less than five minutes and was made in silence. By the time they arrived, Victoria's sister-in-law had already opened the garage door. Jess and Victoria entered the darkened interior that was mainly used as a storage area and found the other woman wiping the dust off the intricately carved crib.

''Don't worry about cleaning it now,'' Victoria told her. ''I'll do all that after Jess gets the bed set up.''

Maggie, a petite redhead, chuckled wryly. ''This thing hasn't been touched since Aaron was three years old. There was so much dust on it, the wood looked more like pecan than dark oak.'' She made a few more swipes across the footboard, then straightened from her bent position.

"Hello, Maggie, how are you?'' Jess greeted her.

She gave him a warm smile, but Jess could plainly see the sparkle in her eyes was still missing. Six years had passed since Hugh had been gored to death by one of the ranch's bulls. Obviously she still wasn't over the death of her husband and Jess felt deep sorrow for her loss. Maggie had been one of the few people on the T Bar K who had never judged him for leaving San Juan County. Jess would never forget her kindness and he hoped that someday she would find happiness again.

"I'm fine, Jess.'' She rubbed her dusty hands on the back of her jeans. "I'm sorry to hear your daughter is sick. Maybe the crib will help a little.''

"I do appreciate it, Maggie. Thank you.''

Maggie's gaze swung curiously back and forth between her sister-in-law and Jess. No doubt she was wondering if the two of them had picked up their affair again, Victoria thought ruefully.

The notion filled her with uncomfortable heat and she cleared her throat, then said, "I guess it would be wishful thinking to ask if you had any crib sheets around.''

Her expression thoughtful, Maggie tapped a finger against her chin. "It's possible. While Jess loads the bed, do you want to come in and help me search through the linen closet?''

Victoria glanced at Jess. "I'll only be a few

minutes," she promised. "And we do need the sheets."

He waved a hand at her and Maggie. "Go ahead. I'll load the bed and wait for you in the truck."

Inside the quiet house, Victoria glanced around for her young nephew. "Where's Aaron?"

"He went to a friend's house this evening after school. They'll be bringing him home soon," she said as the two women made their way down a long hallway to the east end of the house.

Victoria wrinkled her nose with disappointment. She'd always been close to her nephew, but since Aaron had reached the ripe old age of nine, he was getting more and more involved with activities outside the ranch and that meant Victoria got to see him less and less.

"Well, maybe it's best he's not here right now. He'd want a hug and I'd hate to pass Katrina's scarlet fever to him."

"Don't worry," Maggie assured her. "I won't let him come over to the big house until your little patient has gone home."

They reached the linen closet, where Maggie opened the door, then turned a keen eye on her sister-in-law. "Jess still looks the same, doesn't he? Except maybe a little more filled out. A little better."

Victoria's gaze fell to the floor rather than let her sister-in-law read anything in her eyes. "I hadn't noticed."

"Hmm. That would be impossible for any red-blooded woman not to notice. And you never were good at lying, Victoria. Everyone else might believe you're over the man, but I don't."

Maggie was the same age as Victoria and from the very first day Hugh had brought her into the family, the two women had become like sisters. Maggie was well aware that Jess and Victoria had planned to marry and move on to the Hastings ranch. She also knew how deeply in love Victoria had been with Jess at that time. Even so, Victoria didn't want to admit to Maggie, or even to herself, that she was still in love with Jess Hastings.

"This isn't about Jess and me," Victoria said bluntly. "His daughter is ill. That's all there is to it."

Maggie rolled her eyes toward the ceiling. "So you say. But I can't remember you bringing home any patients in the past."

Frowning at the other woman, Victoria tried to defend her actions. "I didn't bring this patient home. She was brought to me."

With a knowing smile, Maggie began to search through a stack of colored sheets. "That's true," she blithely agreed. "But you could have sent her to a hospital."

"I could have. But you wouldn't want Aaron to be hospitalized unless it was absolutely necessary. Jess feels the same way about Katrina."

"He has family, Victoria," Maggie pointed out.

The only thing keeping Victoria from getting angry with her sister-in-law was that she knew Maggie wasn't protesting her decision to care for Katrina here at the ranch. She was only trying to prove the point that Victoria was doing a special favor for Jess. And in Maggie's eyes that could only mean Victoria still cared for the man. Well, that was okay if Maggie wanted to think that way, just as long as Jess knew the truth.

"He has grandparents," Victoria granted. "But they have their hands full taking care of the Hastings ranch. They don't need the stress of taking care of a sick baby."

Tilting her head back, Maggie surveyed the shelf above her head, then stepped back out of the way. "You're taller than me. Take a look on the top shelf."

Rising on tiptoe, Victoria thumbed through the stacks of linen until she reached a printed fabric that looked as though it belonged in a little boy's nursery. "Here's something with teddy bears on it," she announced. "And another with dogs."

"That's the crib sheets," Maggie said with a wan smile. "I kept all of Aaron's baby things because Hugh and I planned to have more children. But then…well after he was killed I gave most everything away. I guess I hung on to the crib for sentimental reasons." Her little laugh was full of sadness. "Apparently I forgot about having the sheets. That tells you how often I clean out this closet."

With the sheets safely down from the shelf and tucked under one arm, Victoria turned to her sister-in-law and gently scolded, "You sound like your life is over, Maggie. You're still a young woman. You'll have more children some day."

Shaking her head with firmness, Maggie closed the closet door and motioned for Victoria to precede her down the hallway. As the two women walked, she said, "I can't imagine letting myself get that intimate with another man, Victoria. Just the idea—" pausing, she shuddered, "—leaves me cold."

"That's only because you haven't met the right one," Victoria insisted.

Maggie shot her a fatalistic smile. "And I always believed Jess was the right one for you. Maybe we're both destined to live alone."

Victoria's eyes darkened with sadness. "I hope not, Maggie. Life is too short to live it without love." Trouble was, the only love she wanted was Jess's.

Once the two women reached the door leading out to the garage, Victoria swiftly pecked a kiss on Maggie's cheek.

"Thanks for letting me use these things," she told Maggie. "Once Katrina goes home, I'll get them back to you."

"No hurry. Like I said, I won't be having any need for baby supplies. Maybe you will," she added slyly.

A hollow pain pierced a spot between Victoria's breasts. At one time she'd needed the baby things. But the little life growing inside her had been lost. For over four years now, she'd carried the secret of her miscarriage without any of her family or friends knowing. And the thought of it never failed to cut her swift and deep. She could only wonder what, if anything, Jess might have done back then if he'd known she'd been carrying his child.

With a mental shake, she reminded herself that was all over and in the past. It was useless to agonize over what might have been.

"I wouldn't hold my breath waiting for that to happen," Victoria tried to joke, then with a wave of her hand she left the house and hurried to Jess's waiting truck.

* * *

Later that night, Jess woke with his heart pounding and a sense of foreboding smothered him like a heavy blanket of smoke.

Jerking upright, his eyes searched the shadows dancing across the strange walls. Where the hell was he? Something was wrong.

Adrenaline surged through him, instantly clearing his mind of sleep. *Katrina.* She was ill. But she was getting better. Victoria was taking care of her.

With a ragged sigh of relief, he reached up to rake the tousled hair off his forehead. As his hand came in contact with damp skin, he realized he was sweating. From his dreams, he supposed. The temperature in the room was comfortable.

Tossing back the cover, he slipped quietly to the bathroom where he splashed cold water onto his face and chest, then dried off with one of the thick towels Victoria had supplied for him earlier.

A glance at his wristwatch told him he'd been asleep three hours. He'd not expected to sleep at all. In fact, he'd only gone to bed because Victoria had insisted. And once she'd taken Katrina to her bedroom, there'd not been much sense in staying up alone. But now the need to see his daughter and re-assure himself that she was all right had him reaching for his jeans.

Victoria's room was across the hallway at a slight angle from his. He walked the short distance quietly, then paused on the threshold as he took in the sight of Victoria sitting on the side of the bed.

Wearing only a thin white nightgown, she had Katrina cradled in her arms. He could hear her humming a lullaby as she rocked his daughter in a gentle, soothing motion.

Jess's first intention had been to knock and make Victoria aware of his presence. But that plan was swiftly forgotten. There was something about the heavy swath of dark hair falling against her cheek, the glow of the night-light on her face and the image of his daughter cradled against her breast that touched something deep inside Jess.

He didn't want to feel it. Or even admit that there was such a place inside him. And he fought to push the unwanted emotions away as he stepped into the room.

Spotting him, Victoria put a shushing finger to her lips, then rising from the bed, she placed Katrina back in the crib.

After pulling a light cover over the toddler, she moved away from the crib to meet Jess in the middle of the room.

"How is she?" he whispered.

Victoria gestured toward the open doorway. "Let's step out in the hall so we won't disturb her."

Jess inclined his head in a motion for her to precede him. Brushing past him, Victoria paused at the foot of the bed long enough to grab her robe.

Out in the hallway, she pulled on the silky white garment while Jess watched, a mocking twist to his lips.

"I don't know why you're bothering with that thing," he said while eyeing the clinging robe. "You were already covered."

Victoria shot a brief glare over his naked chest. He'd always had the fit body of an athlete and the

sight of his hard muscled flesh decorated with a dia-
mond-shaped pattern of curly brown hair made her
feel like she was sinning just by looking.

"Well, you're certainly not," she snapped.

He shrugged as though her accusation meant little
to him. "So? We've seen each other with much less
on than this."

Unable to meet his gaze, she drew in a shaky breath
and crossed her arms over her breasts.

"I've been trying hard to forget that, Jess. I was
hoping you already had."

If there'd been even the slightest hint of sarcasm in
her voice Jess would have found it easy to give her a
brash retort. But there was none. The only thing he
heard in her words was a lost, quavering sound that
twisted the cords in his throat to tangled knots.

Soberly, he said, "I can't forget something that
beautiful, Victoria. Not as long as I'm alive."

Stunned by his admission, her gaze jerked up to his
face. And a strange, terrifying thrill rushed through
her as she realized he was speaking the truth.

Her hands began to shake and her mouth went dry
as the strong urge to reach out and touch him fought
with the rationality of keeping her distance. It
wouldn't do for her to start wanting Jess Hastings
again. But then, had she ever really stopped, she wondered wildly.

Clearing her throat, she said, "Katrina woke a few
minutes ago and began to whimper for you."

"Why didn't you wake me?" he asked anxiously.

"Because I thought you needed to rest," she answered simply. "And she didn't fuss for long. I managed to get her to use the potty and drink a whole cup

of water, so that's encouraging. Along with the fact that her fever is minimal.''

She was changing the subject to Katrina, Jess noticed. But that was okay with him. He needed to be reminded of why he was here on the T Bar K. Rather than remembering the past and this woman he'd once loved.

''You don't know how much of a relief it is to hear you say she's improving.''

A faint smile curved Victoria's soft lips. ''Oh yes. I think I do.''

He released a long, pent-up breath, then pushed a hand through his hair. Victoria watched a short sandy lock fall carelessly over his forehead. Maggie was right, she thought, Jess hadn't changed. He was still just as potently masculine as the first day she'd met him. And judging from her weak-kneed reaction to him, maybe even more so.

His gray eyes flickered over her face, then moved completely away to a spot in the darkened hallway. ''Uh—I managed to get a little sleep,'' he said. ''I can sit up with her now, while you get some sleep.''

Victoria shook her head at his offer. ''I expect Katrina to sleep for several hours now. Besides, I'm a doctor, remember. I'm used to getting only snatches of sleep.''

''And I'm a lawman,'' he pointed out wryly. ''I'm used to having my sleep interrupted.''

''Well, there's no sense in either of us losing sleep while your daughter is resting,'' Victoria reasoned.

And there was no sense in him standing here aching to put his hands on her, Jess thought with a measure of self-disgust.

"You're right," he said brusquely. "I think I'll get a drink and head back to bed. That is, if it's okay to prowl in Marina's kitchen after hours."

Her dark brows drew together at his notion that they lived so formally here on the T Bar K. "Of course it's okay. Help yourself to anything in the refrigerator or pantry. On second thought," she added, motioning him to follow her down the hallway. "I'll come with you and show you where everything is kept."

To be in Victoria's company any longer than necessary was like tempting a person on a diet with a hunk of apple pie. Especially with the two of them secluded in a quiet house, in the middle of the night and no one around except his sleeping daughter. But he could hardly refuse to join her without making himself look like a fool.

The long hallway was dimly lit at regular intervals with muted night-lights. Without speaking, Jess walked alongside her until they reached the kitchen. Then he waited in the middle of the darkened room until Victoria flipped on a light over the range and another over the table. As his eyes adjusted to the brightness, he tried to look at anything and everything but Victoria.

Walking to the huge refrigerator, she said, "Marina usually keeps the place stocked with juices, milk and soft drinks. Or if you need caffeine I can make coffee or tea."

He hardly needed caffeine. The sight of her in thin, silky lingerie was more than enough to set Jess's heart to pounding.

"Plain water is all I need," he told her.

With her back to him, she pulled out a jug of orange

juice. "I would say you're an easy man to please. But I happen to know better."

He walked over to where she stood by the cabinet counter. Stopping a few inches from her left shoulder, he realized too late that he was close enough to catch the alluring scent of her hair and skin.

"Show me where the glasses are," he muttered. "That's all I need to please me right now."

Pointing to the cabinet door directly in front of him, she said, "You'll find a glass there. And bottled water in the fridge, if you'd rather have it."

Scowling now, he jammed the glass under the tap. "Do I look like the bottled water type?"

No, Victoria thought, as she fought to keep her eyes off the naked expanse of his chest. He looked like a man who wanted everything raw and in its natural form. Especially women.

"Just offering," she said.

Pouring herself a glass of juice, she carried it to the pine table and sank onto one of the long benches that served as seating. Before she'd taken two sips of her drink, her eyes began to betray her. As they dwelled on his broad shoulders and lean waist, her thoughts wandered back to the time when it would have been natural to go to him and put her arms around him, to kiss his lips and whisper how much she wanted him. But all of that had ended between them and she needed to forget.

"You know," she said quietly, "it's been a very long time since you've been here in the house like this."

Swallowing most of the water, he turned to look at

her. "What do you mean 'like this'? I was here a couple of weeks ago."

Her nose wrinkled. "That was in the capacity of undersheriff. You're not a working lawman now. At least, not at the moment."

His eyes fell to the squat glass in his hand. One thing about Victoria, she'd always respected his job and his desire to be a lawman. She'd never tried to take that away from him. He had to give her credit for that.

"No. I'm not working as undersheriff right at this moment. Nor will I be while I'm here on the T Bar K."

The faint lift of her brows was barely discernible. "Exactly what are you trying to say?"

His gray eyes zeroed in directly on hers and Victoria's heart thumped at the intimate connection.

"I'm trying to say that as long as I'm here with Katrina I won't take advantage of your hospitality to gather information on your family members or ranch hands."

That he thought it might even be necessary to gather information on the people closest to her was a chilling reminder that he was a peace officer first and foremost.

Closing her eyes, she shook her head. "I guess I should be thankful for that much."

Seeing the anguish on her face, he moved around the table and took a seat opposite her. "Look Victoria, I'm not saying that this is only a pause and that once Katrina is well I'll be back here on the ranch deliberately digging for clues. It might be as you said the other day. The man simply fell and the whole thing was an accident. For everyone's sake, I'm hoping that's what the coroner's report will state.''

She opened her eyes to search his face and was shocked to find no mockery or sarcasm behind his words. It was the first time since the body had been discovered on the ranch that she'd heard him talk this way. ''You sound as if you really mean that.''

He shrugged. ''Why shouldn't I? Just because I'm a lawman doesn't mean I want a case to turn out to be foul play. In fact, the opposite always makes my job easier.''

A troubled sigh slipped past her lips. ''Yes. But in this case we're talking about the Ketchums. And I…know how you feel about us.''

Jess suddenly found it was easier to study the scars on the pine tabletop than to face the faint accusation in Victoria's eyes. It was true, he'd always disliked Tucker, but he didn't have anything against the rest of the Ketchums. Except her and the fact that she'd broken his heart.

''Do you honestly think I would be here with my daughter if I thought that badly of you?''

Moments passed without a reply from her. Jess lifted a questioning gaze to her face. She pressed moist lips together and thrust a hand through the heavy swath of hair dipping over her eye. As he watched the silken strands slide against her neck, he thought about all the times he'd seen those dark waves fanned out on a pillow, all the times he'd thrust his fingers into the shiny mass as he'd kissed her lips.

''I'm not sure what to think anymore, Jess. Why did you bring Katrina to me?'' she asked softly.

Her blunt questions caused him to shift in the chair

and clear his throat. There were several logical reasons he could point out to her, but none of them really described his motive for bringing Katrina to the T Bar K, he silently reasoned. In truth, he wasn't sure what had prompted his sudden decision to grab up his daughter and head straight to Victoria. The moment he'd laid eyes on his feverish daughter, he'd been gripped with fear. All he could think was that Victoria would know exactly what to do to make his baby girl all right again.

The idea that he still needed this woman, even in the capacity of a doctor, thinned his lips to a hard, uncompromising line. "Look, Victoria," he said finally. "If you're expecting some sort of admission from me, forget it."

Disgusted with his hot-and-cold attitude, she rolled her eyes. "The question I asked you is very simple. It doesn't require a confession from you."

"Confession," he repeated with sarcasm, then mouthed a curse word for good measure. "I'm not harboring any thoughts about you that you don't already know about. As for bringing Katrina here, I—" He let out a rough breath, then rubbed a hand over both sides of his jaws. "I wanted her to have the best care. And I knew you were the one to give it to her."

Once the words were out, he felt like a fool. Especially when she continued to stare at him for long moments. But then suddenly a soft smile tilted her lips and her hand slid across the tabletop until her fingers were touching his.

"That's all the reason I need to know, Jess."

Chapter Seven

"Daddy come home?"

Victoria gazed down at the golden-haired toddler in her arms. Three nights had passed since Jess had brought the sick little girl to the ranch. Since then the antibiotics had worked wonders. Katrina's temperature was now nearing normal and the red rash, which had covered two-thirds of her body, was beginning to fade and disappear.

With a gentle smile, Victoria attempted to reassure the child. "Your daddy will be here soon."

Awkwardly, Katrina scrubbed her tearful eyes with both fists and pushed out her lower lip. "I want Daddy," she mumbled.

Victoria was amazed that a child who was only a few months past two years old could have such an inner radar about her father. As soon as late evening began to approach, Katrina was convinced it was time for her daddy to come home.

"Would you like to go look out the window to see if he's coming?" Victoria asked, hoping the action would pacify the child for a few minutes.

For an answer Katrina eagerly bobbed her little head up and down.

Victoria rose from the rocker and, with the child carefully cradled in her arms, walked out to the living room, where a large picture window gave a bird's-eye view of the long winding driveway leading up to the ranch house. However, dusk had already fallen to shroud the road with long shadows. If Jess did appear soon, all that Katrina would be able to see would be headlights.

But that didn't seem to matter to Katrina. Her whines stopped instantly the moment Victoria eased them both down in a big armchair facing the window.

"Daddy come home?" Katrina repeated the question, only this time her round gray eyes were filled with excitement instead of tears.

"Yes, little angel, I'm sure he'll be home soon. So we'll sit right here and wait on him." And hopefully he'd show up before midnight, Victoria added silently.

Years ago, Victoria had seen firsthand that Jess's job as a peace officer was just as unpredictable as a doctor's. Unexpected emergencies and heavy caseloads made his workdays long and exhausting. But she'd learned something new these past evenings as she'd sat with Katrina and waited for Jess to appear. She was just as eager as his daughter to see the man.

Which was crazy. Jess hated her. He still blamed her for their breakup. And after four long years, it was pretty clear he wasn't going to have a change of heart about her. Yet, none of that seemed to matter. When he walked through the door, the sight of him filled Victoria with a joy she could hardly contain.

Sighing wistfully, she gently ran her fingers over Katrina's red-gold curls. The baby was already becoming a part of her. Which was a mistake, she knew. Yet try as she might, she'd not been able to keep her emotions separated from the child. And it wasn't because Katrina was a patient, she silently reasoned. Victoria had treated endearing little patients before and managed to keep her heart from overtaking her head.

No, this time Victoria had to face the fact that Katrina wasn't an ordinary patient. She was Jess's child and that was all it had taken to steal her heart.

Two hours later, at the sheriff's office in Aztec, Jess leaned back in the desk chair and flexed his stiff shoulders. A glance at the clock on the wall told him he'd worked far longer than he'd intended. But at least the overtime had enabled him to catch up on all the paperwork he'd been putting off for the past several days.

Rolling his shoulders again, he raked a hand through his hair. Victoria had probably been expecting him to show up at the ranch hours ago. By now she was probably worrying why he wasn't home yet. He'd called much earlier to let her know he'd be late but Marina had answered the phone and he couldn't be sure the cook had passed his message on to Victoria.

Jess's lips twisted as he gathered the papers he'd been working on and shuffled them into one neat pile.

Who was he kidding with that kind of thinking, he wondered. The T Bar K was the last place that would ever be his home. And as for Victoria, she'd quit waiting and worrying about him years ago.

A light knock suddenly interrupted Jess's thoughts and he looked toward the open doorway to see Chief Deputy Daniel Redwing, his shoulder resting casually against the doorjamb. The younger man had changed out of his uniform and into civilian clothing and was obviously headed home for the night.

"You're burning the midnight oil, aren't you, boss?"

Jess shrugged. "I could say the same for you. I didn't know you were still here."

Daniel pushed away from the doorway and stepped into the room. "We just finished working that break-in down at the tire shop."

"Any suspects?"

"No one definite. But we've got some good prints." Daniel inclined his head toward the papers on Jess's desk. "Have you gotten the coroner's report back on the T Bar K case?"

Jess shook his head. "Not yet."

"I wondered if you still wanted me to do that interview with Maggie Ketchum? Or have you already done it yourself?"

Sighing, Jess wearily pinched the bridge of his nose. "Since Katrina and I have been staying on the ranch, I haven't questioned anyone out there. I—I didn't think it would be...playing fair, so to speak. But that doesn't mean that the investigation is off by any means. Once I take my daughter home, I intend to pick it right up again."

The deputy's brows lifted. "You sound as though you expect this thing to turn into something more than just an unidentified corpse."

Jess frowned. "I didn't say that."

"You didn't have to," Daniel replied. "I could hear it in your voice."

With a wry smile, Jess rose to his feet. "Then I guess I'm going to have to watch how I say things. I didn't realize I was getting transparent."

He reached for the Stetson hanging on a peg by the door and jammed the brown felt hat onto his head. Daniel stepped back and waited for him to shut the office door, then the two men walked together down a short corridor leading to a back exit of the building.

"You're not transparent, Jess. I just happen to know you pretty well. And I know how your mind works."

Victoria knew him pretty well, too, Jess thought. He hoped to hell she hadn't been reading his thoughts. Otherwise she would know these past three days his thoughts had been consumed with her and wanting to get her into his bed.

"Well, just between me and you," Jess said, "I have an uneasy feeling about this John Doe. Nothing adds up to where the body was found."

"I don't suppose you've implied such a thing to Victoria," Daniel said sagely.

Jess snorted with mocking disbelief. "She already believes I'm biased against the Ketchums."

The two men stepped outside to a small parking lot used only by employees of the sheriff's department. At the bottom of a small set of steps, Daniel paused and glanced over at Jess.

"Well, you are, aren't you?" he asked. "Biased, that is."

Surprise arched Jess's brows as he studied the younger man. "Hell, Redwing, you know I'd never tamper with evidence. One way or the other."

Daniel chuckled. "I didn't mean you were biased as a lawman. I meant personally. You never liked the Ketchums. Or has that changed these past few days?"

Jess frowned. It wasn't like Deputy Redwing to bring up personal things. But the two men had been friends for a long time and no doubt the other man was probably surprised that Jess had swallowed his pride and asked Victoria for help.

"If you're wondering about Victoria and me, then quit. The only reason I'm staying out at the T Bar K is to get my daughter well."

Daniel's expression turned serious. "That's too bad. I was hoping you two could put the past behind you."

Daniel Redwing was not a family man. Nor was he a romantic. In fact, Jess had long ago quit trying to figure why the younger man avoided women. So it was surprising indeed to hear the deputy make such a comment about Jess's love life or lack of it.

Starting toward his truck, Jess tossed over his shoulder, "You'd better stick to investigating crime, Redwing. And as for Maggie Ketchum, I'll let you know when I want you to question her."

A half hour later, Jess stepped wearily into the dimly lit ranch house. Instantly his gaze zeroed in on the sleeping woman and child in the armchair. Victoria's head had tilted toward her right shoulder. A thick curtain of black hair had slipped to cover one eye and cheek. Even in sleep her hands were cradling Katrina's back, keeping the child cuddled safely to her breasts.

For long moments he continued to stare at the picture of his daughter and the woman he'd once loved. The two of them shouldn't look so right together, he thought. Victoria wasn't Katrina's mother. She never would be. Yet looking at them now, he could only wonder how different their lives might have been if Victoria had given birth to his daughter.

Don't think about it, he told himself. Tucker Ketchum would have never let them be happy. He would have done his best to have total control over his daughter and granddaughter. The old man would have caused a war between Jess and Victoria and ruined their marriage before it even got started.

No, Jess fiercely told himself, he'd done the right thing by leaving New Mexico. Yet, as his footsteps slipped quietly toward the woman holding his baby, there was an empty ache snaking its way through the middle of his chest.

The moment he touched Victoria's shoulders, she stirred and looked up at him. As her eyes focused on his face, her lips formed a soft smile that went straight to his heart.

"So you finally made it home," she said.

Surprised by the sudden thickness in his throat, Jess glanced away from her drowsy green eyes and swallowed. "Yeah. I had a lot of paperwork to catch up on. I hope Katrina hasn't been giving you a lot of trouble."

"Not really. She watched for you until she couldn't stay awake any longer."

He glanced back at Victoria, then down at his daughter. "I'm sorry I couldn't get here earlier. But I'd put off a stack of paperwork for as long as I could." His eyes softened with fatherly love as they slipped over Katrina bundled in her favorite pink pajamas. "She's okay, isn't she? She hasn't taken a setback?"

Victoria shot him a censured look. "You called three times today and each time I assured you she was improving. You know I would have called you if anything with her had changed."

She was right, of course. He'd put Katrina's health into Victoria's hands. It only stood to reason that she wouldn't keep him in the dark about something so important.

"Yeah, I know you would," he admitted. "It's just that I can't help being worried."

A look of understanding crossed Victoria's face. "Katrina is still improving. The antibiotics are doing their job and her fever is low-grade. I expect by tomorrow it will be gone completely."

"Then she'll be ready to go back home?"

The eagerness in his voice cut her. Which was silly. Just because she'd been enjoying his company, didn't mean he'd been liking his stay here on the T Bar K.

Drawing in a deep breath, she tried to push away the dark thought. "Not so quick," she told him. "Your daughter will still need a few days of recuperation."

Jess wanted to argue and tell her he needed to be out of this house and away from her. But he couldn't. To do so would be a slap in the face after all the wonderful care she'd given Katrina. Plus, it would reveal to her just how much being around her was affecting him. And dear Lord, it was affecting him. In all the wrong ways.

"Well, whatever it takes to make her well," he said, then reached to take the sleeping child from her arms. "I'll carry her back to the crib for you."

Victoria placed Katrina in his outstretched arms, then followed him down the hallway to her bedroom. When he placed Katrina in the crib, the little girl squirmed, but after a few moments settled back into a sound sleep.

"Has she eaten and taken her medicine?" Jess asked as he tucked a light blanket around Katrina's shoulders.

Victoria watched his fingers touch his daughter's forehead, then brush at the curls surrounding her face. The same fingers that had once touched her with such passion. And at the time, Victoria had believed he'd been touching her with the same sort of love he was bestowing upon his daughter. But she'd been wrong about that. And so many other things, she thought sadly.

"She ate with me earlier. And she's already had her medication for the day. She'll probably sleep all night now."

Jess nodded. "Good. I'll be up in the morning to spend some time with her before I leave for work."

He turned away from the crib and Victoria dimmed the small lamp on the nightstand at the head of her bed. As the two of them left the room, Victoria said, "There's not many men as devoted to being a father as you are, Jess."

He arched a cynical brow at her. "Is that a compliment coming from you, Tori?"

Heat seeped into her cheeks, forcing her to glance away from him. She didn't know why he came out with that nickname from time to time. She'd told him not to use it. Surely he understood it made her think of all those occasions when they'd made love, when he'd whispered the shortened name in her ear. Or maybe that was exactly why he continued to use it, she thought wryly. Maybe he was trying to make her remember and hurt.

"Just stating the obvious, Jess. If you want to take it as a compliment, then you're welcome to."

By now they'd reached the end of the hallway and she gestured toward the entrance to the kitchen. "Have you eaten anything?"

"No. But I can find myself a sandwich or something."

She flashed him a compliant smile. "I'm sure you can. But I left the remains of our supper on the cookstove and since it was venison steak I figured you might be interested."

"Last night pot roast, tonight venison steak. Marina's outdoing herself for me," he joked, knowing full well the woman had only half-forgiven him for leaving Victoria behind and going to Texas to become a border patrol agent.

"Marina loves to cook. Even when there's not a man around," Victoria assured him.

Inside the kitchen, Jess unbuckled the holstered .45 revolver from around his hips and placed the weapon in a safe spot atop the refrigerator. Beside the pistol, he rested his worn Stetson. At the same time, Victoria pulled a clean plate from the cabinet and began to fill it from the pots and pans on the stove.

"Don't worry," Jess replied with amused acceptance. "I know Marina's efforts aren't for my benefit. If she thought she could get away with it, she'd probably take pleasure in poisoning me."

Victoria placed the plate of food in the microwave and punched in a short amount of time. Once the steak and vegetables were heating, she turned to look at him.

"Marina doesn't hate you. And she could never harm anyone. She's a loving woman."

His expression turned serious as he walked over to where she stood waiting by the microwave. "Marina serves me because she considers it her job," he said. "But I hardly expect you to wait on me, Victoria. Go sit down."

He was standing so close she could smell the lingering scent of cologne on his clothes, see the faint lines fanning from the corners of his gray eyes, the red-gold highlights threaded through his hair and all the other little things about his face that she'd once fallen in love with.

Suddenly her heart was beating wildly and the urge to reach out and touch him was taking over her thoughts. Quickly, before she made a fool of herself, she murmured, "I'll go make coffee."

"I can do that, too," he said as his gaze fell from her eyes to her lips. The house was too quiet, he thought. Marina had obviously retired to her own living quarters and Katrina was out for the night. Ross was still away on a business trip. Jess and Victoria were alone. And the last thing he needed was for her to be treating him like a husband who deserved the attention of a devoted wife.

"No doubt you can," she said abruptly as she headed to the cabinet counter. "But this way I can make it the way I like it."

The bell on the microwave sounded and Jess turned his attention to retrieving the warm plate of food. Once he was seated at the table, he picked up his fork and began to eat, but it was only a matter of moments before he was glancing over at Victoria, watching her movements as she went about putting the coffee makings together.

Tonight she was dressed casually in worn jeans and a peach-colored cotton sweater. The sleeves were short and the neckline scooped low in the front and the back. Her pale skin gleamed like soft satin in the muted light of the kitchen. Her midnight dark hair was piled in a messy knot atop her head and the stray tendrils curling against her neck, tempted him, reminded him what it was like to put his hands in all that silky hair and hold her head fast as he kissed her lips.

What in hell was wrong with him, he wondered. Why did his thinking go so haywire whenever he was around Victoria? Four long years had passed since he'd touched her. Really touched her. Any sane man would have already gotten over the woman. But in spite of the passing time and a marriage that had failed from the get-go, he'd not been able to erase Victoria completely from his mind.

Needing to break the grip on his thoughts, he forced himself to speak. "I suppose staying home...away from your medical practice has been boring for you this week.''

She glanced over her shoulder at him. ''Not in the least. I've had Katrina to keep me busy. And I'm never bored here on the ranch.''

He focused his gaze on the food in front of him rather than on her. For a long time before he'd ever met Victoria, he'd known about the beautiful Ketchum girl. From time to time, he'd seen her at a distance around town and each time her grace and beauty had quietly bowled him over. In his mind, she'd been an unattainable princess, who'd never look sideways at someone of Jess's caliber.

Yet when he did finally meet her, he'd been surprised to learn she wasn't the stereotypical ''rich girl.'' She wasn't a party person, or a big shopper or a globe-trotter. She had simple tastes and a love of ranching life. Her only ambition was to help people. All those things had led Jess to believe the two of them were compatible, that she really could love someone like him. But then he hadn't counted on Tucker's interference. Not at first.

''Pa said you didn't start your medical practice until after Tucker died. He said you stayed here on the ranch and cared for the old man. Is that true?''

Victoria poured water into the coffeemaker. ''Yes, that's true. After you left for Texas, his heart grew steadily weaker. He needed daily medical attention.''

He considered her words for a moment. ''You Ketchums have never lacked money. Couldn't you have hired a live-in nurse?''

With the coffee dripping, she walked over to where he sat at the pine table. ''We did hire a nurse. But after the fifth one quit, Ross and I both realized it was hopeless.'' She made a helpless gesture with her hands. ''You know how Daddy was. Particular and demanding. None of the nurses could please him. They'd do something he didn't like and then he'd get all worked up and yell and throw things. The situation was putting added stress on his heart. I eventually decided the only choice was for me to care for him myself.''

His expression knowing, he glanced at her. ''And put your life on hold.'' Again, he wanted to add.

She grimaced. ''I didn't think of it that way.''

''No. You wouldn't.''

Stepping closer, she looked down at him, then clasped her hands together. As though she was trying to curb the urge to touch him in some way. The idea heated his blood like a shot of raw whiskey.

''Look Jess, I know that if your Pa needed your help you'd be the first to give it to him.''

He nodded. ''Of course I would. I'd do anything I could to help him. But not give up my career as a lawman. He wouldn't expect or want that from me.''

Jess watched her eyes slowly search his face and was surprised that he saw no accusation in the green depths. Instead, for the first time he could remember, she was looking at him as though she really wanted to understand his way of thinking.

''And you believe Tucker wanted me to put off my career as a doctor?'' she asked softly.

Jess took a deep breath and let it out slowly as he considered Victoria's question. He didn't want to argue with her. God knew she'd pulled his baby back from a horrible fever and he was very grateful for all she'd done for the both of them. Yet he couldn't lie about his feelings on a matter that had ultimately torn them apart.

Slowly, he swallowed a bite of the venison then said, "I believe Tucker wanted you to put off anything in your life that would take you away from him. Especially me."

Color filled her cheeks. "That doesn't make sense, Jess. He had Ross. And Hugh, before he got killed. There wasn't any need for him to be so possessive of me."

"You're right. There wasn't any need for it. The man had a thriving ranch, plenty of money and a family that surrounded him with love and attention. But *you* were his little girl, his sunshine." Just as she'd been Jess's sunshine, he thought. And once they'd parted, the world had been a much darker place for him.

If Jess had been throwing the words at her in an accusing way, Victoria would have found it easy to be insulted, to hurl accusations right back at him. But he wasn't angry or blaming. He was quietly stating the facts, the way he'd seen them. Had she been blind back then, she wondered, or had he? Had Tucker purposely clung to her just so she wouldn't leave with Jess? The mere idea that she was even asking herself such a question left her feeling like the floor was tilting beneath her feet.

Walking back over to the cabinet, she poured two mugs full of coffee and carried them back to the table. Sitting across from him, she took a careful sip of her drink, then said with quiet reflection, "I can't deny that I was Daddy's favorite. I don't really know why.

He loved his sons. Losing Hugh to that horrible accident in the bull pen was very difficult for him. Then mother died, too, and I guess he felt like his world was crumbling around him. That's when he started to…cling to me. But obviously you saw all that. All I saw was a parent who needed me.''

Jess had tried so hard to open Victoria's eyes to the ways of Tucker. But he'd never been able to make her see the old man was a user. He'd cheated on his wife, then pretended to be heartbroken when she'd died. Yet each time Jess had tried to point this out to Victoria, she'd accused him of being selfish and cold-hearted. Now, hearing her admit to being so blinded back then was like gouging open a wound that had never quite healed.

Releasing a heavy breath, he said, ''Yeah. I know.''

She reached over and covered his hand with hers, jolting Jess with the unexpected touch. ''Do you really, Jess?'' she asked softly. ''I never believed you understood back then. And I'm not sure you do now.''

The needy look in her green eyes made him so uncomfortable he had to drop his gaze back to his plate. ''I don't think we ought to go into this tonight, Tori. It only dredges up bad feelings for both of us and we don't need that. At least, I don't.''

''No. I don't want us to argue. But ever since you left for Texas, I've wondered what happened to us. I wanted you to stay here with me…more than anything.''

Her raw, husky voice made him want to believe her. And maybe he did to a certain point. But the truth was she'd not wanted him enough to leave New Mexico and Tucker behind.

Cursing as he felt himself softening to her touch and the lure of her words, Jess told himself it didn't matter what she was saying or how good it felt to have her hand on his.

In a voice gone suddenly gruff, he said, "I wanted a lot of things, too, Victoria. But I didn't get them."

As soon as his words died away, the room went unbearably quiet and her hand slowly pulled away from his. From the corner of his eye, Jess watched her rise to her feet and as she walked out of the room, the heavy thudding of his heart seemed to match her footsteps on the Spanish tile.

Lifting his head, he let out a weary breath. He'd not wanted to hurt her. But damn it, he couldn't get sappy over her again. Not now. Not ever.

Chapter Eight

For the next hour, Jess tried his best to push Victoria completely from his mind. After he finished eating and clearing away the dirty dishes, he checked on Katrina, then went to his bedroom and took a shower. Yet all the while he tried to busy himself, the quiet emptiness of the house began to close in around him.

Eventually, he prowled through several rooms on the pretext of hunting for something to read. When he failed to find Victoria in any of her usual places, he went out to the back porch where several pieces of lawn furniture were scattered across the planked floor.

Although it was dark, there was enough moonlight to allow him to pick up her silhouette sitting in a cushioned glider at the far end of the ground-level porch. As he walked over to her, he told himself he was definitely a glutton for punishment. He didn't need to be out here. There was no reason for it. Except that where Victoria Ketchum was concerned, he couldn't seem to help himself.

"What are you doing out here?" she asked with faint surprise.

Not waiting for an invitation, he eased down beside her. "I could ask you the same thing."

She sighed and he wondered if the sound was an expression of pleasure or if it had been made out of the sheer weariness of dealing with him.

"I'm enjoying the warm night," she answered his question. "We don't have very many of them, you know. At least not here in the mountains."

The fact that her voice was warm and welcoming made him feel like a heel. Although Jess didn't know why. Earlier, in the kitchen, the only sin he'd committed was speaking truthfully. He couldn't help it if she didn't like what he had to say.

"It's pretty obvious that you're trying to avoid me," he said.

Turning her head, she looked at him in the semi-darkness and was amazed at how just the sight of his profile still had the power to make her ache with longing.

"You made it clear I was talking too much. So I thought it best to stay out of your way for a while."

He rubbed a restless hand against his thigh. "You were talking too much," he admitted. "But," he shrugged as he searched for his next words, "I didn't mean to sound so…sharp."

Pressing her lips together to keep them from trembling, she glanced away from him. In a husky voice, she said, "Yes, you meant to."

Sheer frustration caused him to groan loudly and her eyes to sweep back to his twisted features.

''Victoria—'' he began only to have her soft voice interrupt him.

''Please don't start apologizing. Especially when you really don't mean it.''

But he did mean it, Jess thought. Hurting Victoria, even with just words, was something he no longer wanted to do. When and how that had happened, he didn't know, but he was certain about one thing—the change scared the heck right out of him.

''Why are you making this so damned hard, Tori? Just what do you want from me?''

The question caused Victoria to writhe with pain. At one time in their lives, he'd known exactly what she'd wanted from him. His touch, his love, his children and the promise that he would love her until their dying days. But she supposed he'd forgotten those days when he'd professed to love her. Back when the two of them had planned to marry and build a house of their own on the Hastings ranch. She knew he didn't want to hear those sorts of things from her now. The thought made her throat tighten painfully until her voice was little more than a hoarse whisper when she finally answered, ''You don't really want me to answer that, Jess.''

His eyes roamed her shadowed face. ''What makes you think so?''

She reached for his hand and slid her fingers intimately between his. Unwittingly, the image of the two of them naked, their bodies entwined, flashed through Jess's mind and his heart began to pound with hot, needy anticipation.

"Because you still blame me for everything that happened between us," she answered in a quiet, matter-of-fact way. "Because you...don't want me...the way I want you."

He muttered a curse word. "Are you crazy, Tori? Do you know what living under the same roof with you these past few days have been doing to me? It's all I can do to keep from getting up out of my bed and crossing the hall to you."

For long moments Jess could feel her eyes searching his face. Then suddenly, before he knew what was happening, her arms were sliding around his neck and her lips hovered next to his.

"Then why haven't you, Jess?"

Like a flash of lightning, white-hot desire was suddenly surging through his body, stirring his blood to a heated frenzy. With a mind of their own, his hands slipped to her shoulders. His brow leaned into hers. "Don't do this to me, Tori. To us," he whispered roughly. "You'll only be sorry."

Her fingers pleated together at the back of his neck and pressed into the strong muscle and bone. "I've been sorry before."

The delicious warmth of her body, the flowery scent of her hair and skin, the touch of her fingers were all luring him, tugging him to a place he shouldn't go. Yet it was impossible for him to pull away from her, from all the things he'd hungered for since the two of them had parted.

"Damn it," he murmured in a low, agonized voice, "this is crazy. It's not going to get us anywhere. But, right at this moment I don't really care."

Her response was a sigh and a kiss so soft that it

only whetted his appetite to have her. With a deep groan of surrender, he pulled her against him and slanted his lips roughly over hers. Instantly her mouth opened, inviting his tongue to slip inside. As he tasted that intimate part of her, his hands slid beneath the hem of her sweater and stroked the soft skin of her back.

Victoria's head reeled with hot sensations as she was suddenly thrust back to all those years ago when Jess had been her man, her love. The taste of his mouth, the searching pressure of his lips, the hard warmth of his body was all just as wonderful as she remembered and her heart was suddenly weeping from the sheer joy of touching, loving him again.

By the time he finally lifted his head, her pride and common sense had flown away into the dark night. She clung to him tightly, her fingers dug into his back as she pleaded, "Oh Jess, make love to me."

He eased his head back far enough to look into her eyes. Indecision flickered in the gray depths and she realized he was fighting a mental war with himself. He wanted her, yet he hated himself for it.

As moments passed, she began to fear he was going to reject her, but then his head bent back to hers and he gave her a kiss so hungry and forceful it stole the breath from her lungs.

As she struggled to regain her lost air, his hot gaze roamed her face. "Just remember you asked for this," he said thickly, then quickly rising to his feet, he tugged her up from the glider.

With her hand gripped tightly in his, she followed him through the maze of lawn furniture until they reached the back door. There he paused and pulled her into his arms long enough to kiss her again.

The urgency and need Victoria tasted on his lips stoked the fires already burning inside her and she quickly began to unfasten the buttons on his shirt. When she parted the heavy cotton and smoothed her hands over his heated skin, he groaned and grabbed her fingers.

"We can't do this here," he said huskily.

Taking her by the arm, he led her into the house and down the long hallway to his bedroom.

At the side of the bed, he quickly removed her clothing, pausing long enough between articles for a kiss here, a touch there.

Beneath the urgency of his hands, Victoria's heart pounded with a mixture of pleasure and unbearable anticipation. For four long years her sexual needs had gone into cold hibernation, but now Jess was here, bringing her desire back to a bright, burning flame. She couldn't touch him, taste him enough. And the banked glow in her eyes told him so.

He removed his own clothes in hasty jerks. Once they were heaped on the floor in a pile next to Victoria's, he settled her back onto the mattress, then stretched out beside her. As he took her into his arms, memories were showering his mind, filling him with a longing so deep it shook his hands and pained the very center of his heart.

Pressing kisses along his jaw, she murmured feverishly, "Oh Jess, Jess. This is the way we were always meant to be. Tell me I'm right."

He closed his eyes against the beauty of her face.

"Nothing about this is right, Tori. But God help me, I want you. I can't stop wanting you."

"Jess—"

Whatever else she'd been going to say was blotted out by his lips. After that, all words were forgotten as his fingers reacquainted themselves with her breasts, her belly and thighs, and eventually, the warm, wet silkiness between her thighs.

Of all the times he'd imagined making love to Victoria again, he'd always done it in slow motion. He'd taken the time to explore every inch of her, to stoke the fires in both of them until the heat of wanting was unbearable. But now that he had her for real, he couldn't slow his movements or the rushing need to have her completely.

Sensing his impatience, she ripped her mouth away from his and panted, "Don't wait, Jess! I need you now!"

He lifted his head just enough to look at her. "Are you sure?"

Wrapping her legs around his, she lifted her hips invitingly against his bulging arousal. "Oh—oh yes," she choked. "Make me yours. Again."

Jess didn't need a second invitation. He slipped the hard length of his arousal inside her and their bodies began to move in a frenzied reunion.

Victoria wasn't sure if minutes or hours had passed when she finally floated back to earth. Her lungs were heaving and sweat bathed every inch of her skin. Her hands, which had been gripping Jess's back just moments earlier, were now as limp as her sated body.

Eventually, her breathing slowed and her strength returned. Jess was still draped over her and with a contented sigh, she lifted a hand and began to stroke his shoulder. But after a few moments Jess moved himself off her and rolled to one side of the mattress.

Turning her head, she looked at him with soft drowsy eyes. Making love with Jess again had felt like coming home from a long, lonely journey and in the process she'd learned what she'd feared for the past four years. Jess was the only man she could ever want. Ever love.

With the back of his arm resting against his forehead, Jess raised his gaze toward the ceiling. "What is the matter with us, Tori?"

The hollowness to his question widened her eyes and stung her with fear. Had nothing changed? He'd just shaken the earth beneath her. Hadn't he felt anything?

"Nothing is wrong with me," she said carefully. "I feel wonderful."

She would, he thought bitterly. As long as Victoria Ketchum got what she wanted everything was wonderful in her eyes. But then how could he fault her for what just happened between them? Jess asked himself. He'd gotten what he'd wanted, too, hadn't he?

Expecting him to take her into his arms as he'd always done when they had made love in the past, Victoria rolled toward him and waited.

But this isn't the past, Victoria. And Jess isn't exactly that same man who used to make love to you.

Across from her, Jess twisted his head so that he was facing her. There was nothing soft about his expression or his voice as he said, "I don't know what you think this means, Victoria, but I don't intend to let you make a fool of me again."

She stared at him while the rosy glow that, only moments ago had been warming her heart, now changed to ice-cold fingers of disbelief.

"Is that..." she swallowed as emotions threatened to overwhelm her. "Is that what you think I was trying to do?"

Jess's jaw hardened even more as he steeled himself not to let his eyes dip from her face. He couldn't allow his gaze to linger on her beautiful, naked body. Not when desire for her was already building in him again like a monster out of control. Damn her. And damn himself for being so pitifully weak.

"I don't know what your motives are," he said lowly. "I just want to make sure you understand I have no intentions of getting involved with you, or any woman. Ever again."

Victoria wasn't a naive teenager with her head in the clouds. She wasn't silly enough to believe that one physical connection between them was suddenly going to make him fall in love with her. Or even make him want to have an affair with her. Yet she had expected him to be, if nothing else, warm and tender toward her. Apparently he was incapable of showing her even that much, she thought sadly.

Feeling the sudden need to cover her nakedness from his eyes, she reached for the side of the bedspread and pulled it over her entire body.

"There's no need for you to insult my intelligence, Jess. I didn't expect this to prompt a marriage proposal from you."

Outwardly, her voice was cool, but underneath Jess thought he heard the hint of a tremor in her words. Or maybe he'd imagined that part. Maybe he wanted to believe she wasn't as composed as she appeared. Especially when making love to her had shaken him right to the very core of his being.

"I just wanted to make sure…my feelings are clear to you."

She breathed deeply and hoped the burning pain between her breasts would go away. At the moment it was practically unbearable, like a hand clawing away her flesh layer by layer.

"Oh, don't worry, you've made your point, Jess. And you've made it clear how you feel about me. What I don't understand is why you've decided to exclude women from your life. Don't you ever plan to give Katrina a mother?"

The mention of his daughter made Jess inwardly wince. Of course he wished Katrina had a mother. There were many things he would never be able to do for his daughter. Not the way a mother could. But he'd tried love with Victoria and marriage with Regina. The two failures had convinced him that women were not to be a part of his life. Not if he expected to live it with any sort of peace of mind.

"No."

The blunt answer had her searching his embittered expression. "It's easy to think that Katrina will always stay a toddler like she is now. But believe me, it won't be long before she's going to need maternal guidance."

Straightening his head on the pillow, he focused his gaze on the foot of the bed. "Ma was a good mother to me. She will be for Katrina."

Victoria raised up on her elbow as she studied him with disbelief. "Alice is a wonderful woman and no doubt she's a good role model for Katrina. But your grandmother is no spring chicken, Jess. As much as you'd like to think it, she won't be around forever. How is she going to keep up with an energetic teenager?''

"Don't concern yourself about it, Victoria. I'll see that my daughter is raised in the right way.''

He was shutting her out, Victoria realized. But that was nothing new. Not after four long years without so much as a word from him.

"By depriving her of a mother?'' she couldn't help but ask.

He shot her a mocking glance. "Is that what getting me into bed with you was all about? Are you auditioning for the role of Katrina's mother?''

She was crazy, she told herself as she tossed back the bedspread and reached for her clothes. Jess didn't want her love or concern. All he'd ever wanted from her was sex. She'd known that for years now, yet her head couldn't seem to convince the rest of her body.

As for being the mother to Jess's child, he'd never realize just how much she'd once wanted and expected to be just that.

"I must have sucked in too much night air,'' she muttered with self-accusation. "I'd forgotten what a bastard you can be.''

He watched her leave the bed and snatch up her clothes from the floor. As she bundled them into a ball in her arms, the look on her face told him she was furious and hurt. He'd accomplished what he'd set out to do. But the fact did nothing to ease the emptiness inside him.

"Yeah. Just like Tucker used to be,'' he said flatly.

She glared at him, then turned and left the bedroom.

Once she was out of sight, Jess went to the bathroom and stood beneath a cold shower for several long minutes. But the second he stepped out, the sight of the bed and the memory of Victoria's giving body heated him all over again.

It was going to be a hell of a night, he thought miserably.

Two evenings later, Victoria was sitting with Katrina on the living room carpet. Spread out before the two of them was a pile of building blocks and an assortment of tiny trucks and cars that Maggie had saved from Aaron's early childhood. The toys weren't exactly what Victoria would have chosen for a little girl, but Katrina appeared to be enthralled with each piece.

A few feet away, in a stuffed armchair, Maggie sat sipping iced fruit juice. "You look exhausted, Victoria. Has Katrina been keeping you up at night?"

Surprised by Maggie's remark, Victoria glanced over at her sister-in-law. "Why no, she's been sleeping soundly. And I'm not exhausted. I just look that way because I'm not wearing makeup."

"I noticed."

Victoria's brows arched with wry speculation. "What does that mean?"

Maggie waved a careless hand in Victoria's direction. "Not what you think. You don't need makeup to be beautiful. But when I see you without a trace of lipstick, I know you must be *really* tired."

Victoria sighed. "I'm not tired, Maggie. I've just

een very busy. I'm not used to taking care of a
hild.''

Maggie let out a dry laugh. "No, you're just used
o taking care of two dozen patients a day.''

Victoria felt a tiny hand patting her leg and looked
own to see Katrina holding up a miniature pickup
uck.

"Daddy drives twuck,'' she said, giving Victoria a
oothy grin.

Her heart full, Victoria affectionately ruffled the
oddler's sandy blond curls. "That's right, sweet
ning.''

"I drive twuck, too. See, Toria?'' Katrina pushed
ae toy across the carpet while making the *brrring*
ound of a motor.

"I think your little patient has recuperated,'' Mag-
ie commented.

Yes, Katrina was well, Victoria thought, and she
vas thrilled the child had recovered so nicely. Yet her
lossoming health meant there was no longer any rea-
on for Jess and Katrina to continue their stay on the
anch.

The thought of not having Katrina in her day-to-
ay life was casting a long shadow across Victoria's
eart. And Jess. How could she get by without seeing
is face, hearing his voice? Making love to him again
ad reawakened all her hopes and dreams, reminded
er just how much he'd always been a part of her. But
is cold treatment afterward had told her he wanted
o part of a future with her in it.

Her eyes felt grainy and hot. She closed them
riefly as she replied to Maggie's comment. "Yes,

Katrina is well enough to go home. I suppose I'll have to tell Jess tonight."

The other woman carefully studied Victoria's downcast face. "You don't sound too thrilled about it."

Victoria glanced once again at her sister-in-law. "I'm very happy Katrina has her health back. It was terrible to see her so lifeless with fever."

"But you don't want her to go home," Maggie stated the obvious.

Victoria's lips twisted ruefully as she gazed at Jess's daughter. "I…" she stopped, sighed, then started again, "No. To be honest she's starting to feel like my own child."

Even though Victoria wasn't looking her way, she knew Maggie slowly shook her head with disapproval. "That's not a good thing, Victoria. You're a doctor and a good one. You know you can't get emotionally attached to a patient."

"Katrina isn't just a patient," Victoria pointed out. "She's…well, she's Jess's child."

Maggie's expression was suddenly all knowing. "Ahhh," she said softly. "So it's still like that."

Before Victoria could reply, Katrina climbed into her lap. Smiling, she bent her head and kissed the child's baby-soft cheek, then made her giggle by running her fingers lightly across her belly.

"You know, Maggie," Victoria spoke wistfully, "for a while after Jess left, I told myself I hated him. That was the only way I could survive without him. But now—"

"You realize you never really hated him," Maggie gently concluded.

Victoria cast the other woman a wry glance. "No. The moment I saw him again I realized…I was in trouble."

Confusion flickered across Maggie's face. "Why do you say that? Jess is single now and you're unattached. There isn't anything stopping the two of you from getting back together."

Only the fact that Jess didn't want her or love her, she thought sadly. Two nights ago he'd made it painfully clear how he felt about her. There was no sense in her being delusional and hoping his heart would change.

Katrina suddenly decided to drive the little truck to a different spot on the wide expanse of carpet. With the child out of her lap, Victoria rose to her feet and walked over to the picture window that looked down upon the twisting driveway and a part of the barns and work pens. As usual, the ranch yard was busy with cowboys tending to animals, unloading square bales of alfalfa hay, and spreading cattle cubes in long troughs in the feedlots.

For a few moments she studied the busy sight without really seeing it, then finally she spoke in a heavy voice. "Jess doesn't want the two of us…to get back together, Maggie."

Maggie frowned. "Why not? You two were planning your wedding when he got that border patrol job. I'm sure he cared for you very much or he wouldn't have wanted you to be his wife."

"Hah," Victoria retorted bitterly. "Jess didn't care about me four years ago and he doesn't care now."

"I think you're wrong," Maggie said. "He was wildly in love with you back then."

Bitter tears burned Victoria's throat. "So why did he leave and marry someone else?"

Maggie sadly regarded her sister-in-law. "Don't tell me you haven't really thought about it. Surely you know that it was important for Jess to be his own man. It was only natural that he wanted a better job. He wanted it for you and for him."

Victoria shook her head. "I didn't want money or things from Jess! Dear God, I already had all of that! Jess was irreplaceable. He was the most precious thing to me!"

"He wanted to be able to give you financial security. Not have Tucker do it for him!"

Victoria looked at her. "He hated Daddy. Jess thought Daddy looked down on him. But that wasn't true. Daddy would have given him a job. We could have all been together and happy."

This time Maggie shook her red head. "I'm sorry to say this, Victoria, but I think it's time I did. Tucker was my father-in-law, and maybe that's why I saw him from a different angle. In any case, he would have never allowed you to marry Jess. You were his darling. No man would have been good enough and especially not one who made his living as a city cop. And Jess was smart enough to know this."

Victoria groaned as hopelessness and regret hammered her from every direction. "You're probably right, Maggie. And I—well, I've made a horrible mess of things. I've hurt Jess too much for us to ever have another chance at being together. And now Katrina has—" she paused and glanced sorrowfully over her shoulder at the curly haired child playing on the floor. "She's become my little girl."

Maggie's head continued to swing back and forth in dismay. "I don't know what to say."

"Why not say the obvious?" Victoria asked ruefully. "I'm a fool. A woman without common sense. I'm not fit to be a doctor. I can't even take care of myself, much less someone else."

Rising from the armchair, Maggie crossed the room and took Victoria by the shoulder. "Don't talk that way. You're a brilliant woman. You've helped countless people in San Juan County. And many of them were without money or health insurance. If not for you, most of them would have remained ill or died. I don't want to ever hear you degrading yourself like that."

"But Maggie—"

Maggie threw up her hands in exasperation. "Victoria, you're not a fool! You're a woman in love."

Biting her lip, Victoria glanced away as tears stung her eyes. "Yes," she agreed. "In love with the wrong man."

Later that night Victoria was curled up on a couch in the study when she heard footsteps moving through the house. Jess was finally home, she thought, as she gripped the medical journal she'd been trying to read.

Lifting her gaze to the open doorway of the room, she listened to the *clunk, clunk* of his cowboy boots and waited while her heart pounded faster and faster.

He wouldn't come looking for her, she reminded herself. For the past two nights he'd avoided her like the plague. Last evening the weather had been unusually warm and he'd carried Katrina down to the bull pen so that she could see the animals. Victoria had not been invited to join them. The evening before that he'd come home late and, finding Katrina already asleep, mumbled something about being tired and had gone straight to his bedroom.

As for herself, Victoria had tried her best to appear cool and unaffected by his aloof attitude. She'd already humiliated herself enough by begging him to make love to her. She wasn't about to add to that humiliation by letting him see how much she wanted to be near him, talk to him, touch him.

Sighing, she tried to refocus her attention back on the newly released report on diabetes. Moments later Jess's deep voice sounded from the doorway and she jerked with a start.

"Sorry to interrupt you," he said coolly. "Since Katrina was already asleep for the night, I wanted to check with you about her day. Is she all right?"

Tossing the journal aside, Victoria rose to her feet and walked over to where he stood just inside the room. With her heart continuing its erratic pounding, she allowed her eyes to travel slowly over his tired face, then to slip down his lean, hard body.

A khaki shirt with the San Juan County sheriff's department emblem on the sleeve was tucked into a pair of well-worn Wranglers. Belted around his waist was the .45 he carried while on duty. With his dusty hat and boots and the badge pinned over his heart, he looked no different than the lawmen who'd long ago worked to tame the Wild West.

"Your daughter is fine," she assured him. "She had a good day."

He grimaced as his eyes caught hers. "I suppose

you've been thinking my job keeps me away from my fatherly duties way too much."

When Victoria had first met Jess, she'd quickly learned that he was dedicated to enforcing the law. It was in his blood, just as being a doctor was in hers. She'd always respected his desire to protect and serve his fellow man. It was just too bad he didn't feel as passionate about her as he did about being a lawman.

"I'm sure there're times it can't be helped," she said stoically. "I've never faulted you as a father."

He lifted his Stetson and smoothed a hand over his streaked hair. As she watched his simple movements, longings of the most basic kind shot through her and she took a deep breath and glanced away from him.

"A deputy was involved in a high-speed chase this evening. A drunk driver trying to avoid a DUI," he explained. "Another officer and myself had to join him and help throw up a block to stop the car. It was late before we finally managed to make the arrest."

Surprise pulled her eyes back to his face. "I thought as undersheriff, your job was more administrative than—in the line of fire."

His mouth twisted into a wry grin. "I wasn't in the line of fire, Victoria. It was just a car chase."

She couldn't believe how casual he was about the whole thing. "That's just as dangerous as someone with a gun!"

One of his broad shoulders lifted and fell. "There isn't a lawman in San Juan County who simply sits behind a desk."

And Jess had never been a man to sit back and let someone else do the tough jobs when he could do them himself, she thought.

''I don't like to think of you—in harm's way.''

She said it without really meaning to and as his eyes narrowed on her face, she could feel her cheeks turning red.

His hands came up to rest on the front of his holster. ''Don't tell me you worry about me, Tori. I wouldn't believe it.''

Of course she worried. Any man that wore a badge was a target for criminals and maniacs. ''I'm not heartless, Jess. I'm a doctor. I worry about anyone who jeopardizes his or her life.''

Mockery turned down the corners of his lips. ''So your concern is just an impersonal, medical thing. I should have known.''

It was far from impersonal, Victoria thought. But she wasn't going to admit such a thing to him. His ridicule of her feelings was too hard to take.

Lifting her chin, she said briskly, ''I'm glad we're speaking now, before you retired for the night. I have something to tell you.''

His brows arched upward. ''You make it sound important.''

The effort to remain cool while he was so temptingly near was making her whole insides shake. ''It is. It's about Katrina.''

Concern quickly narrowed his gray eyes. ''You told me she was doing well.''

Her throat was suddenly so tight she had to swallow before she could form one word. ''She is. That's why I wanted to speak with you. To tell you that your daughter is now well enough to go home.''

Jess stared at her. He should be shouting for joy,

he thought. Instead, he felt as though an axe had just fallen on him.

For the past three days he'd tried his best to push their lovemaking out of his mind, but he'd failed miserably. All he could think about was having her soft lips and warm body beneath his. Each time the memories of that night entered his mind, his body began to burn with need. Each time he came near Victoria, he had to fight with himself to keep his hands off her.

He needed to get off the T Bar K and away from her. He needed to get back on the Hastings ranch where he belonged and forget that anything could or might ever be between him and Victoria.

"Obviously you couldn't wait to tell me," he said, his voice tinged with sarcasm. "Should I wake Katrina and leave now?"

Her jaw clamped together as she struggled to stop herself from calling him an ugly word. "That's uncalled for, Jess. Especially when you know how much I care about Katrina. I love having her here. There's no urgency for you to leave anytime soon. You can stay as long as you'd like."

Releasing a heavy breath, he looked away from her and shook his head. "You know that's impossible, Tori."

The raw emotion in his voice surprised her, stung her heart with bittersweet longing. "Why? You don't have to worry that I'll beg you to make love to me again."

His face whipped back to hers and he stared at her with a measure of disgust. "Damn it all, Tori, what makes you think I need to be begged?"

Chapter Nine

The air around them was suddenly crackling with electricity. Victoria was certain some of it had arced straight to her heart and short-circuited its wiring. It was beating out of control, sending blood singing in her ears.

"I thought…these past few days you've made a point of keeping your distance," she told him.

He grimaced as though he couldn't believe he had to explain his actions. "Hell yes, I've stayed away from you. I had to. Otherwise we'd have been right back in bed together. You ought to know that!"

He still wanted her. That shouldn't mean anything to Victoria. Not when his wanting was driven by sex. Yet her body was already reacting to his words, even though her mind was screaming at her to back away and end their conversation.

''What happened between us the other night felt right, Jess. You can't deny that,'' she said hoarsely.

He stepped closer and, if possible, her heart beat even faster.

His eyes glinting with sexual messages, he whispered, ''No. I won't deny it. But *feeling* right doesn't necessarily make it right.''

Her nostrils flared as the scent of his warm, male body enveloped her senses. ''Since when did you get so righteous?''

Jess's gaze continued to slip over her face and the cloud of dark ebony hair surrounding it, then moved downward over the lush curves of her body. Tonight she was wearing a dress of pale pink cotton. The neck was scooped low, while the tiny row of buttons down the front of the bodice made his hands itch to unfasten the material and expose her breasts. The rosy brown nipples would be hard with excitement, he thought. And the taste of them would be almost too sweet to bear.

Trying to shake away the intoxicating thought, he said, ''I'm not talking about morals, Victoria. Our being together is crazy. We'd only wind up hurting one another.''

The overwhelming need to touch him suddenly overrode her pride and she slid her hands up his hard chest until she could latch her fingers over the tops of his shoulders.

''You're hurting me now, Jess.'' With catlike grace, she stepped forward and arched her body against his. ''By *not* making love to me.''

His brain silently shouted at him to move away from her, but his body wouldn't have any part of the order. Before he could stop himself, he bent his head and roughly covered her lips with his.

The taste of her was like a potent shot of whiskey that sent a jolt of heat shooting from the top of his head to the soles of his feet. It dulled his senses to everything but the need to ease the craving that had burned in the pit of his stomach for the past three days.

Moments later, when the need for air finally forced him to lift his head, he muttered, "You're a damned temptress, Victoria. And I'm weak. Too weak for my own good."

Desperately she searched his face for some sign of gladness that she was back in his arms. But all she found was a passion so dark it made her shiver against him.

"What does that mean?" she asked in a strangled voice.

He closed his eyes and slid his hands around her waist. "It means I can't resist you. Not now. Not tonight."

But he would afterwards, she thought, as he led her down the hallway to his bedroom. Later, after his passion for her body had cooled, he would walk away from her. And once he was gone from the ranch, the temptation for her would be over. Yet knowing all of that was not enough to make her deny herself the pleasure of his body.

Hours later Victoria was stretched out close beside Jess on the tousled bed, but she felt as though the small space separating their bodies was as wide as a mountain canyon. Like before, their lovemaking had been hot and urgent. But as soon as it had ended, Jess had moved away from her, both physically and mentally.

Now as her eyes slid over his silent, stony profile, her heart ached so badly she wondered how it could keep on beating.

"I didn't know sex with a woman could make a man so unhappy," she teased in an attempt to lighten the awkward tension that had suddenly settled around them.

Jess's head turned toward hers. "This shouldn't have happened," he said flatly.

Anger hot and swift, spurted through her. "I sure wasn't twisting your arm!"

"No. You use more subtle tactics than strongarming."

Disgusted with him, she made a move to scoot off the mattress, but before she could swing her legs over the side, Jess reached out and caught her by the wrist.

One of her brows arched in question.

"You're not leaving yet," he said. "I want to—there's something I need to say."

She studied his face in the semidarkness as she imagined how different, how sweet this moment might be if he truly loved her. He would take her into his arms and tell her that the two of them were meant to be together, that he didn't want to live without her.

But he didn't love her, she reminded herself. She supposed she'd ruined all of that years ago when she'd decided to remain in New Mexico with her ailing father. And now she would never hear such words of love from Jess.

"There's no need for you to say any more

about…what just happened between us,'' she said stiffly. ''I know how you feel.''

Did she, Jess wondered. If so, then she knew a hell of a lot more than he did. Right about now he felt lower than a snake in the grass. He wasn't a user. He despised anyone who was. Yet he'd used Victoria to assuage his own sexual desires. Not once, but twice.

You didn't use her. You made love to her. Love.

The whispering voice inside him came from out of nowhere and momentarily shocked him. He'd loved Victoria once. But not now, he mentally argued with himself. Never again was he going to be foolish enough to trust his heart to any woman. Especially this one.

''I'm glad you do,'' he finally managed to say. ''Because I don't want you to get any wrong ideas about this and think I've changed my mind about…us.''

Pain wrapped around her heart and filled her chest with a heavy weight. ''I wouldn't dream of it.''

Her clipped reply caused his fingers to tighten ever so slightly around her wrist.

''Look, Victoria, I'm not going to deny that I want you. God knows I just showed you how much. But I'm not stupid enough to think that something permanent could ever work between us. There's too much bitterness for us to push aside. Besides that, you're a Ketchum, a doctor. You have a successful practice in Aztec. You don't need a man in your life, especially a poor one like me.''

Astounded by what she was hearing, she jerked away from his hold on her wrist. ''You're right, Jess, I don't need you for money. There's other things a woman wants much more, like companionship and love. Or have you lowered everything between us to just sex?''

Jess felt so sick inside he had to look away from her before he could speak. ''Don't ask me for love, Tori. I'm not capable of loving any woman again.''

She slid away from him and climbed off the bed. Thankfully, the room was full of shadows and he couldn't see the tears blurring her eyes as she began to gather up her clothes.

''And I'm not capable of giving myself to a man who's only interested in my body. So I guess we might as well call this night our last.''

''Might as well,'' he replied, but the words were so low and strained Victoria didn't hear them as she headed out the door.

The next morning before daylight, Victoria woke to the scent of strongly brewed coffee.

Glancing groggily to her left, she was surprised to see Katrina gone from her crib. Apparently Jess had come into the bedroom at some time during the night or early morning and gotten his daughter. Had the two of them already left the ranch?

Tossing back the covers, she quickly wrapped a robe over her gown and hurried out to the kitchen.

Relief swept over her as she spotted Jess sitting at the table with Katrina perched on his knee. Even though he didn't glance her way, she could tell by the faint stiffening of his shoulders that he sensed her presence in the room. So it was going to be that way, Victoria thought sadly.

At the gas range, Marina took a moment away from flipping pancakes to glance over her shoulder.

"Morning, *chica*," she greeted Victoria. "You up early."

Marina was studying her with a mother's shrewd eye and Victoria realized she must look awful. Normally, she took the time to brush her hair and splash cold water on her face before she came to breakfast. But this morning was different. This morning Jess and Katrina were leaving and her heart had never felt so heavy.

"I—have a lot scheduled today," she lied while hoping the woman couldn't guess she'd spent the greater part of the night in Jess's bed. "I needed to get an early start."

Smoothing a hand over her hair, she moved to the cabinet. With a barely audible sigh, she picked up the coffee carafe from its hot plate and filled a cup, then added a large measure of rich cream.

At the table she took a seat kitty-corner to Jess and Katrina. The moment the child spotted her, she reached out for Victoria to hold her.

"I wanna eat, Toria."

Still avoiding eye contact with Victoria, Jess said to his daughter, "You'll eat in a minute. Marina has to cook it first. Don't bother Victoria."

"She's hardly a bother," Victoria assured him. "Let me hold her."

Turning slightly, he lifted Katrina over to Victoria. As he did, his gray eyes connected with hers and the intimate contact jolted him with white-hot memories of last night.

Having her in bed with him again had been like

returning to paradise. He could still feel her soft skin beneath his fingertips, hear her faint moans as his body had thrust into hers. Dear Lord, why did he have to want her so, he wondered sickly. She'd already proven to him once that she didn't love him. He'd be the biggest fool in San Juan County if he let himself start thinking he was important to her.

"She's been whining to eat for the past fifteen minutes," he said stiffly. "I guess that's a sign she's over the scarlet fever."

Grateful for the child's warmth and affection, Victoria hugged Katrina tightly. "It's the best sign."

He picked up his coffee cup. "Ma and Pa will be glad to get her back home. They've missed her."

Victoria's throat tightened. For the past five days Katrina's presence had turned the ranch house into a different place. Giggles and squeals and baby talk had filled the silence. Toys scattered over the living room floor had made it seem just that—a living room, not just a space that guests on the ranch sometimes walked through. And her own room, with the beautiful oak crib sitting little more than an arm's length away from her bed, had made it almost seem like she was a real mother. Many times during these past nights, she'd looked over to watch Katrina sleeping peacefully and marveled at how much the baby helped to soothe the raw spots in her heart. But all of that would end today, she thought sadly. And there wasn't a thing she could do about it.

"I'm sure Will and Alice have missed their granddaughter," Victoria murmured around the lump in her throat.

His gaze slipped awkwardly away from hers.

"I...want to thank you again for all you've done for Katrina. It means a lot to me."

Well, at least she meant *something* to him, Victoria thought, then breathed deeply as pain collected in the middle of her chest.

"Like I told you before, Jess. I wanted to do it."

He stared at his coffee cup and as her eyes scanned his profile, she wished she could see inside him, to see for herself if he'd turned hard through and through or if, like her, he was hiding a part of himself.

His fingers twiddled with the handle on his cup. "Well," he said. "Just bill me for what I owe you—for your medical services. As far as I'm concerned, I couldn't pay you enough."

To have him think he owed her, for anything, added a fresh layer of pain to that she already had. Everything she'd done for him and Katrina had been from her heart. "You don't owe me anything, Jess."

Lifting his gaze back to her face, he stared at her in wonder. "You lost a week of work at your clinic, Victoria."

She shrugged. "I didn't become a doctor to make money, Jess."

No, Jess thought, money had never been a priority to Victoria. She'd become a doctor because she'd watched her mother, Amelia, suffer with a rare muscular disorder that had finally taken her life. By going into medicine, she believed she could help the people in her community live longer, happier lives. As for treating Tucker, Jess supposed it had been too late for Victoria to fix the old man's ailing heart. How that must have hurt her.

The realization struck him hard and heavy and he

wondered why it had taken all this time for him to start seeing things through her eyes. Had he been as blind as he'd accused her of being?

"I know that," he murmured. "But I don't expect free medical service from you. I have insurance and—"

"I said I didn't want anything," she interrupted in a tight voice. "Now please don't bring it up again."

He watched her lips compress to a thin line as she bent her head toward Katrina. The whole idea of taking money from him was obviously insulting to her. Although in truth, he'd given her so much more last night as she'd lain in his arms. His very soul had poured into her. But then, she probably hadn't wanted that part of him any more than she wanted his money, he thought ruefully.

"All right," he murmured. "I won't."

Her dark eyes darted over to his face and for a moment, Jess thought she was going to say something. He could see indecision flickering in the green depths, but Marina suddenly arrived at the table with a platter full of pancakes and a pitcher of warm syrup to dispel the moment.

"Is everybody ready to eat?" she asked.

"Eat! Eat!" Katrina shouted while eagerly slapping her palms on the tabletop.

The old cook grinned fondly at the youngster. "I'm glad someone around here appreciates my cookin'."

As Jess forked a few of the pancakes onto his plate, he glanced up at Marina and gave her a fond smile. "I'll miss you when I'm gone, Marina. Maybe you'll miss me, too, huh?"

To his surprise, she patted his shoulder. "Maybe I will, Jess."

Across the way, Victoria blinked as hot tears scalded the back of her eyes. For the past week, she'd started to think of Jess and Katrina as family. Her family. And from the sad look on Marina's face, the older woman had, too.

For the next few minutes, Victoria helped Katrina eat her breakfast. She didn't attempt to down any of the food herself. There was such a hard lump in her throat, it was all she could do just to swallow hot coffee.

Once Katrina had her fill of pancakes, she carried the little girl to the bathroom and gave her a quick bath.

Victoria was sitting on the edge of the tub, dressing Katrina in a pair of small jeans and a T-shirt printed with tiny sheep when Jess appeared in the doorway. Even before she glanced up, she could feel his eyes going over her flushed face and damp robe and she wondered what he was thinking and if leaving was pleasing him as much as it was killing her.

"I have our things packed," he said. "How much longer will it be before Katrina is ready?"

"She'll be dressed in a few moments." She glanced toward the one window in the bathroom to see the early morning sun was just washing away the gray dawn. "Are you leaving this early?"

He focused on the wall behind her rather than her face. "It will give me time to get Katrina home before I have to be at work."

"Oh. I wasn't thinking about your job." She wasn't

thinking about anything. Except that it felt like she was losing him all over again. "I'll hurry this along."

His sober gray eyes drifted downward to Victoria and then to his daughter. The sight the two of them together cut him with a fierce emotion he couldn't, nor wanted, to understand.

In a rough voice, he said, "I'll go put our things in the truck, then meet you in the living room."

Five minutes later, Victoria had Katrina completely dressed and her wet curls combed into a gold-red halo around her head.

"Daddy gone?" she asked as Victoria carried her out of the bathroom.

Suddenly overcome with loss, Victoria paused in the hallway and hugged the child tightly to her breast. "No," she told the child. "Your daddy isn't gone. He's coming back to get you. You're going bye-bye this morning. You're going home."

Unaware of the awful turmoil going on inside Victoria, the child squealed with excitement. "Bye-bye! Daddy take me, bye-bye!"

By the time they reached the living room, Jess was already there waiting. Victoria kissed Katrina's cheek, then lifted her up to him. The little girl instantly latched her arms around his strong neck and grinned happily down at Victoria.

"Go bye-bye, too, Toria. You go, too!"

Victoria was sure her heart was cracking down the very middle as she did her best to smile up at Jess's daughter.

"No darling. I have to stay here. But I'll see you soon." Maybe, she prayed.

Jess moved toward the door. Victoria followed.

"Well—" he began awkwardly, "I guess we'll be going."

She didn't say anything. She couldn't.

Jess studied the toes of his boots. "Thank you again, Victoria. I won't forget all you've done."

And Victoria wouldn't forget the precious moments she'd been in his arms, kissing his lips, giving him the most intimate part of her body.

"Goodbye, Jess."

He carried his daughter out the door. Victoria followed them onto the porch and watched in the early morning light as he situated Katrina in a child's seat, then climbed behind the wheel and drove away.

Chapter Ten

"Jess, you're gonna break that baby's neck puttin' her on a rangy cow horse like Pokie. And after all the trouble Victoria took to get her healthy and well."

Jess glanced over at his grandmother who was standing outside the round horse pen made of wooden posts. For the past five minutes Alice had been watching with an eagle eye while he led the bay horse and his daughter around in a slow circle.

"Pokie wouldn't break anyone's neck," Jess assured her. "Even if a bee flew down and stung him on the rear."

From the seat in her daddy's big saddle, Katrina giggled at the image of Jess's words. "Funny, Daddy. A bee sting Pokie!"

He stopped the horse and with a wide grin reached his arms up to his daughter. "You little stinker, it wouldn't be so funny if a bee did that to you."

The child easily slid from the saddle and straight into her father's arms. The moment he gathered her up, she circled his neck with a tight hold. "Pokie tough, Daddy. A bee won't hurt him."

Yeah, Pokie had exactly what Jess needed, a tough hide. And during the past few years he'd believed he'd developed one. He'd thought nothing could ever get under his skin again. But he'd been wrong. Victoria was like a grub worm burrowing deeper and deeper inside him.

Three days had passed since he'd packed up his and Katrina's things and left the T Bar K, yet he was still haunted by the memory of Victoria standing silent on the porch, her white face strained as she'd watched the two of them drive away from the ranch house.

Even work couldn't take away the tormenting image of Victoria's beautiful face or silence the lingering sound of her voice in his ears. He'd believed coming home to the Hastings ranch would give him relief. Instead he was miserable. He missed Victoria. Missed her like hell. And there wasn't a thing he could do about it.

Crossing the horse pen, he lifted Katrina over the fence and stood her safely on the ground beside Alice. Instantly, Katrina went down on all fours and crawled back under the wooden railing to get to her father and Pokie.

"Oh no, young lady," he said firmly. "You're going in the house with Ma. It's suppertime. The horseback riding is over for today."

"I wanta ride Pokie," she wailed as Jess snaked one arm around her waist.

He plopped Katrina back over the fence and didn't

release her until Alice had a firm grip on her grand-daughter's hand. "Maybe tomorrow if you're a good girl."

Katrina wailed louder. "No. Wanta ride Pokie now!"

"Come along, sweet pea," Alice quickly intervened. "Let's go to the house and you can help me set the table."

As Alice led Jess's petulant daughter toward the house, he took Pokie to the barn to unsaddle him. He found Pa sitting on an overturned bucket inside the tack room and rubbing down a leather bridle with saddle soap.

The older man looked up as Jess lifted the saddle he was carrying onto a wooden rack. "Sounds like Katrina isn't too happy with her daddy," he said with a chuckle.

Jess grunted. "She's getting spoiled. I guess I've let her have her way too often."

"Maybe Victoria did that to her while you two were staying on the T Bar K," Will suggested.

Jess realized he'd blamed Victoria for a lot of things, but Katrina's tantrums weren't one of them. "No. Victoria made her obey. At least while I was around."

Will went back to rubbing the thin strips of leather. "Well, we sure are glad to have you and our grand-daughter back home. It was quiet around here with you gone."

"Yeah, but at least Ma got a rest."

His eyes narrowed shrewdly, Will looked up and studied his grandson's dull expression. "You know, me and your Ma was real surprised that you took Katrina over to the Ketchum ranch. The way you left Victoria all those years ago, we figured you hated the very sight of her.''

Jess sighed. He wasn't in the mood to talk about Victoria, but it appeared as though his grandfather was. After all this time, he could only wonder why. ''I've never hated Victoria. We…just had different priorities in our lives, that's all. And thankfully one of us had the good sense to see that.''

''Hmm. And I guess that was you,'' Will stated thoughtfully.

Jess leaned a hip against a counter piled with horse liniment, shin boots, curry combs and nylon lariats.

''Pa, a man pretty much knows when he's playing second fiddle. It's not a good feeling.''

Will's bushy brows lifted. ''And who was you playin' second fiddle to? I never figured Victoria the kind of woman to look at another man.''

Snorting, Jess picked up a small string of leather and began to tie it in knots. ''It wasn't another man. Not in the sense you're thinking. It was Tucker. She was totally devoted to the old man. She never could see that he was a user. All she could think about was that it was her duty, her place to stay on the T Bar K and hold his hand.''

Will grimaced. ''We're all guilty of using someone, Jess. It's human nature. You can't blame Victoria for loving her daddy. Just think how you would feel if Katrina turned her back on you.''

Jess had to admit it would cut him deeply if Katrina ever turned her back on him. Still, as much as he would always want Katrina to love him, he would never want to dominate her life the way Tucker had tried to control Victoria's.

"Pa, the old man didn't deserve Victoria's devotion. He'd cheated on his wife for years. Hell, I wouldn't tell Victoria this, but she's probably got illegitimate half brothers and sisters scattered all over this state. And there's no telling how many underhanded deals he's made. And with people who were supposed to be his friends. Everyone in San Juan County knew he was deceitful. Everyone knew the T Bar K was built with unscrupulous funds. But Victoria refused to see any of this. Instead, she chose to turn her back on me."

Will sadly shook his head. "Did you ever stop to think you might have put her between a rock and a hard place?"

Jess rolled his eyes, then made a palms-up gesture. "All I did was ask her to go to Texas with me. I wanted to make a life for us. I wanted to take care of her, give her all the things she needed and wanted, instead of her daddy doing it for me. Was that so bad of me?"

After a long, thoughtful spell, Will said, "No. That wasn't bad, son. The bad part is that you've never forgiven her for refusing to leave the T Bar K and go with you."

Forgive her? How was he supposed to do that when just talking about it made Jess's blood boil as though it had happened only yesterday.

"No. I don't guess I have."

Once again Will's head swung back and forth. "You can't forgive her," Will repeated. "But you still love her. That must have you in a hell of a mess."

Jess straightened away from the counter with such a jerk a person would have thought he'd been touched with a live electrical wire. "Where do you get the idea that I love Victoria?"

Will's calm expression didn't change. "It's all over your face, Jess. I can see it plainly."

Will was wrong. Dead wrong. He didn't feel anything for Victoria. Except maybe resentment and regret. And longing. Yes, longing to hear her voice, see her face, hold her soft body next to his. But that wasn't love. It couldn't be.

"There's nothing on my face but a little dust," he told his grandfather. "Now put that bridle away and let's go eat before Ma comes after us."

The next afternoon, Victoria pushed the stethoscope into a pocket on her lab coat and stood back to eye the patient on the examination table. "Your lungs sound terrible, Mr. Morales. You have a pretty good case of bronchitis."

The elderly man looked hopefully at his doctor. "I've been coughing my head off, Doc. Can you make that stop?"

Victoria patted his arm, then reached for her prescription pad. "I'm going to give you something to help with the cough. In the meantime, you're going to need lots of rest and medication to get over this. So I want you to get these prescriptions filled." She handed the small pieces of paper to him. "Now wait right here and Nevada will be in to give you a shot and a list of things I want you to do at home. And I want to see you again in a week. But come in before that if anything worsens, understand?"

Mr. Morales arched a brow at her. "I have to take a shot? Can't you give me some pills to take instead?"

Victoria chuckled. "You're going to get both, Mr. Morales. It will help you get well faster. And don't worry. Nevada has a special touch. You won't even feel it."

Before he could argue that point, Victoria left the examining room and headed back to her office. Once she was behind her desk, she made several notations in Mr. Morales's chart. That finished, she leaned back in the big leather chair and closed her eyes.

She'd never felt so drained in her life. She'd thought coming back to work would make things better and help to get her life back to normal. But so far it hadn't helped her forget how much she missed Jess and Katrina.

"Smile, Doc. Mrs. Guymon canceled right at the last minute so you're finished for today."

Victoria opened her eyes to look at the nurse standing just inside the door of her office.

"That news doesn't make me smile, Nevada. Mrs. Guymon has a heart condition, she has no business canceling her appointment. She did it because she doesn't want me to lecture her about her eating habits."

"You'll have that chance soon enough," Nevada said with a grin. "She rescheduled for tomorrow afternoon."

Sighing, Victoria sat up straight in the desk chair. "Good. So that's it? No one else in the waiting room?"

"All finished. You can go home and relax."

Victoria placed Mr. Morales's file to one side of the

desk and reached for another. "I still have patient notes to catch up on. And going home is…not all that appealing right now."

Her expression thoughtful, Nevada walked over to Victoria's desk. "Are you feeling all right, Victoria?"

Nevada's question brought a look of surprise to Victoria's face. "Why, yes. Why do you ask?"

Nevada grimaced. "Because ever since you've come back to work you've looked strained."

Victoria looked away from the other woman's concerned gaze. "I'm okay, Nevada. I just need a little more time to get back into the swing of working again. That's all."

Nevada's wan smile said she wasn't at all convinced. "You were only off for a week. Maybe you should have taken another week off. Dr. Martinez would have been happy to continue filling in for you."

Victoria shrugged. "I know he would. But there wasn't any need for me to take off work any longer. Katrina had recuperated and Jess was in a hurry to get her back home." And in a hurry to get away from me, Victoria thought sadly.

It had crushed Victoria to watch him and Katrina drive away from the ranch. Yet, hard as that morning had been, the following days had been much worse.

For the past three nights she'd driven home from work and walked into the house, somehow expecting to hear Katrina's squeals and to find Jess at the kitchen table, giving Marina a hard time about her cooking. But of course the house was always silent and empty. As empty as her heart.

A wry smile suddenly spread across Nevada's face. "And here I was thinking that the time Jess was spending on the ranch would bring you two back to-gether.''

Victoria shot her a frown. ''Why would you be thinking such a thing?''

Nevada's grin turned absolutely naughty. ''Close quarters tend to bring two people of the opposite sex together. Especially when they've been lovers.''

Crossing her arms against her chest, Victoria gave the nurse a scathing look. ''I don't feel like talking about this, Nevada.''

''You just told me you felt okay,'' Nevada countered.

Victoria threw up her hands in total despair. ''All right, I'm not okay. I'm miserable. I've fallen in love with a little girl that can never be mine. And I—I wish I'd never seen Jess Hastings again!''

Nevada made a tsking noise of disapproval. ''You don't mean that, Victoria.''

''Why not?'' She asked, her voice rising. ''The man is—'' She stopped as she realized if she said much more, she'd be exposing her feelings.

''One of the sexiest lawmen in San Juan County,'' Nevada finished for her, then with a shake of her head, said, ''No, let me change that to *the* sexiest man in San Juan County.''

Victoria drew in a long breath and heaved it out. ''I can't deny that,'' she admitted to the nurse. ''But he also has to be the most hard-nosed, hard-hearted man in the whole state of New Mexico.''

Nevada's expression quickly changed to one of concern. ''I take it you two parted on strained terms.''

Victoria passed a hand over her furrowed brow. ''I

guess you could put it that way. He was more than ready to leave and I—''

''You're still in love with him,'' Nevada finished flatly.

Dear Lord, was she that transparent? Is that what Jess had seen every time he looked at her? She glanced guiltily at Nevada. ''I wasn't aware I was wearing my feelings on my sleeve,'' she muttered.

Nevada moved around the desk and placed her hand on Victoria's shoulder. ''You're not. It's just that I know you pretty well. And I can see the change in you since Jess and Katrina stayed on the T Bar K.''

Victoria sighed. ''That's just it, Nevada. I don't think I've really changed. Being close to Jess and his child has made me realize that I never stopped loving the man.''

Nevada squeezed her shoulder. ''What are you going to do about it?''

Victoria groaned. ''Now you sound like my sister-in-law, Maggie. And like I told her, there's nothing I can do about it.''

Nevada jammed her hands on the sides of her hips as she studied her boss's wretched expression. ''We're different kinds of women, Victoria. And I probably shouldn't be giving you any kind of advice. But if I loved a man the way you obviously love Jess, then I darn sure wouldn't sit back on my heels and do nothing about it. I'd go after him. Any way I could.''

Shaking her head, Victoria rose from the desk chair. As she pulled off her white lab coat and hung it in a tiny closet at one end of the room, she said, ''Jess doesn't want me going after him.''

"Hah! A man never knows what he wants until a
woman shows him."

Back at her desk, Victoria gathered up an armful of
paperwork then switched off the lamp. "I'll think
about that, Nevada." She glanced at her wristwatch.
An hour until the clinic's usual closing time. Surely
she wouldn't be missed on this slow day. "Now I
think I'll follow your advice and go home. Call me if
you need me."

Outside, the late afternoon sun was very warm, a
warning that hot summertime was growing near. As
Victoria steered her car onto the main highway leading out of Aztec, her thoughts turned to Katrina. She
wished she had told Jess to have Alice bring Katrina
in to the clinic for a checkup. Not that there was much
chance of her having a relapse. The visit would have
merely given Victoria a chance to see the little girl
and hold her in her arms.

A mile passed before another thought struck her.
Jess might not want to see her, but he hadn't said
anything about her staying away from Katrina. And
since Victoria was off early this evening, it would be
a perfect time to stop by the Hastings ranch and see
the child for a few minutes. Jess would be at work,
so there wouldn't be much danger in running into him,
she reasoned with herself.

With her mind made up, Victoria pressed down on
the accelerator and for the first time in days, she
smiled.

A few minutes later Victoria pulled to a stop outside
the Hastings's modest ranch house. As she passed
through the yard gate and walked the short distance

to the front porch, she noticed there had been little
change to the place since she'd last been here four
years ago.

The Hastings ranch had been one of her favorite
places to visit. It was homey and comfortable. Plus,
Alice and Will had always treated her like a daughter.
Much to Victoria's relief, that hadn't changed since
she and Jess parted ways. His grandparents visited her
clinic from time to time with minor health problems
and sometimes she accidentally met up with one, or
both, of them on the streets of Aztec. They always
greeted her with nothing but genuine warmth and affection.

Knowing she would be welcomed made it easy for
Victoria to knock on the Hastings's door.

"Why, it's Victoria!" Alice exclaimed a few moments later as she pushed open the screen door and
folded Victoria into a tight hug. "Oh honey, it's so
good to see you!"

"Hello, Alice. How are you?"

The older woman thrust Victoria out in front of her
and proceeded to inspect her with a shrewd eye. "I'm
fine, honey. Just fine. And you couldn't look more
beautiful."

Victoria blushed at the compliment. "Thank you,
Alice. I hope I'm not disturbing you. I left the office
a few minutes ago and I thought I'd drive by and see
Katrina. Is she here?"

Smiling broadly, Alice took Victoria by the hand
and led her into the house. "She's in the kitchen eating a little snack. I told her to stay there while I answered the door, but once she sees you she's going to
be out of her seat and dancing on her toes. You're

just about all she's talked about since Jess brought her home.''

No doubt that had peeved the man, Victoria thought, as Alice led her through the living room, then down a short passageway, which opened into a large kitchen.

"I've missed her so much," Victoria admitted. "The ranch house has been so quiet without her."

Alice's soft chuckle was full of understanding. "Yeah, kids seem to fill a place with noise. Sometimes I can't hear myself think around here. But I wouldn't have it any other way."

The two women stepped into the kitchen and Katrina looked up from her seat at the small chrome dining table. Her gray eyes grew to saucer size as she spotted Victoria standing beside her grandmother.

"Toria! Toria!"

Like a blur, the youngster slid from her chair and raced straight to Victoria's waiting arms.

With a smile of satisfaction, Alice stood back and watched as Victoria pressed several kisses on Katrina's giggling face.

"See, I told you," Alice said to Victoria. "The little thing has missed you, too."

"I not sick," Katrina announced to Victoria.

Emotion balled in Victoria's throat, making her laugh low and husky. Just being able to hold Katrina again filled her with a pleasure that was indescribable.

"Of course you're not sick," she told the child. "You're all well and strong now."

"Sit down, Victoria," Alice invited, "and I'll get you something to drink. How about a glass of lemonade? That's what Katrina is drinking with her apple slices.''

''Thank you, Alice. That sounds nice to me. All I had to drink at the office this afternoon was a cup of burnt coffee.''

With the little girl's hand safely ensconced in hers, Victoria walked over to the table. Once she was settled into the seat at the end, she lifted Katrina onto her lap.

While Alice prepared the drink, Katrina quickly began to chatter about all that she'd been doing since she'd gotten home. Victoria listened intently and asked questions in all the proper places.

''Sounds like you've been a busy little girl,'' Victoria told her.

Katrina nodded emphatically making her golden-red curls bounce around her face. ''I told Daddy I want to see Toria. He said no!'' She pushed out her lower lip and mumbled, ''I cried and kicked my feet like this.''

The child promptly demonstrated a tantrum and Victoria couldn't decide if she should laugh or cry herself.

''Oh, Katrina, you shouldn't behave that way. Your daddy wants you to be a good girl and so do I. That means you have to be nice, even when he tells you no.''

Alice placed Victoria's lemonade on the table, then drew out a chair opposite her guest.

''We sure are grateful to you for taking care of Katrina all those days,'' Alice said. ''Will and I was so worried when Jess raced out of here with her. She was burning up with fever. I don't think I've ever seen my grandson looking so scared. Funny, isn't it, how a strong, brave lawman can be shaken by such a little bundle.''

Victoria slanted the older woman a wry smile before she looked down at the child in her lap. ''Jess happens to love this little bundle very much.''

''Well, it was a special thing you done. Taking care of her day in and day out like that. You sure saved me a lot of lost sleep.''

''Forget it,'' Victoria urged, then reaching across the corner of the table, she gave the woman's hand a gentle squeeze. ''It's really good to see you again, Alice. How's Will doing?''

She motioned a hand at a door that led out to the yard. ''Oh, he's out riding the back pasture. You can't hardly keep that man outta the saddle. And the little one there, she's just like her daddy and her great-grandpa, she wants to ride a horse eight hours a day.'' Leveling an eye on her great-granddaughter, she added, ''Katrina, why don't you get in your chair and drink your lemonade and then Victoria will have room to drink hers.''

The child wrinkled her nose as though she wanted to argue, but after glancing up at Victoria, she decided it was time for her to be ''nice.''

''''Kay, Ma.''

After Katrina had climbed off her lap and into the chair next to hers, Victoria picked up the glass of lemonade and enjoyed a long drink.

Alice said, ''It seems like old times having you here again, Victoria. We've missed you.''

''And I've missed being here,'' Victoria said truthfully. ''I'm so glad that you and Will didn't turn your back on me after Jess went to Texas.''

Alice snorted. "Just between me and you, we never wanted him to go. But at the time he believed it would help him better himself. And we knew that was important to him."

Closing her eyes, Victoria shook her head with bewilderment. "It's hard for me to understand that he needed to feel better about himself when he was already a hardworking, respectable man."

"Well, I suspect you would've had to have known Jess's daddy, to really understand. The man was my son, but there's no use in me sugarcoating his memory. He was just plain no good. And I guess Jess always felt like he had to prove himself even more to make up for Jim's mistakes."

Victoria frowned. "Jess never talked to me much about his parents. He was so young, only five when his father died, that I figured he didn't remember much about the man."

"He remembers enough, Victoria. And none of it could be pretty, if you know what I mean. Jim was a mean son-of-a-gun whenever he was drinking. And that was just about all the time. It was a good thing Jess was the only child he sired. He wasn't fit to be a father."

Victoria's heart squeezed with pain as she imagined Jess as a child, wanting and needing the love of his father, but getting fear and insecurity instead. It was no doubt why he'd grown up tough. He probably wanted to make sure nothing ever hurt him again. But she'd hurt him, she thought sadly. And she didn't know what to do about it or how she could ever possibly make it up to him.

"What about his mother? I don't suppose you ever hear from her?"

Alice's head swung back and forth. "We have no idea where she went or even if she's still alive now. Jess never mentions her. And me and Will don't bring her up either. It's pretty obvious she didn't want to be a Hastings, 'cause she hasn't ever come back."

"Was Jess close to her?" Victoria asked.

Alice nodded. "The woman was a good mother to him. She sheltered him as best she could from Jim's drunken violence. Will and I were shocked when she left Jess with us. We never could figure why."

Victoria glanced at Katrina who was busily munching on an apple slice. "Well, you and Will have been wonderful parents to Jess. You should feel good about that."

"We do," Alice said. "And we're glad he's back home now."

Bending her head, Victoria stared at the pieces of crushed ice floating at the top of her glass. "I wished Jess had never went to Texas, Alice," she said hoarsely. "I realize it helped him move up the ladder. But, I don't have to tell you that it…tore us apart."

Not known for being subtle, Alice said straight out, "You're a Ketchum, Victoria. Your family has always been rich and well-to-do. That's why Jess jumped at the chance to join the border patrol. He knew he couldn't compete on just a city cop's pay."

He'd often expressed those same sentiments to her, but Victoria had always believed he was just using that as an excuse to lure her away to Texas, away from Tucker.

"I never wanted or needed for Jess to have a lot of

money. That had nothing to do with why I loved him. I made that clear to him many times."

Alice nodded as though this was something she'd always understood about Victoria. "I know. But a man has pride and he was convinced that Tucker considered him low class. And he wanted you to look up to *him*, not your daddy. I imagine you can understand that now."

Yes, she was beginning to understand a lot of things, Victoria thought. She was beginning to see that she'd closed her eyes to Jess's needs and also to her father's subtle manipulations.

"Alice, for years I've heard people talk about my father. About the underhanded deals he made, the fights he'd been in and the women he'd had affairs with. Until recently, I'd always believed that most of those tales had been gossip—fabricated tales about a larger-than-life man who had built a fortune." She shrugged and sighed. "I guess I didn't want to believe they were true and that my father was less than a noble and honest man."

"Of course you didn't want to believe it," Alice gently replied. "He was your daddy. He was good to you and you loved him."

Victoria nodded, grateful that at least Jess's grandmother could understand her motives back then. "Yes I loved him. And even though I've come to the conclusion that he was far from perfect, I still love him. I just wish—" She glanced at Alice. "I wish I'd opened my eyes back when Jess and I were together. I shouldn't have let my father manipulate me like he did."

"You believed he needed you. And I guess he did. He got pretty frail not long after Jess left for Texas."

Victoria grimaced. "Yes, he was in a wheelchair and on oxygen for nearly three years. I guess that was payback for all the wrong he'd done to others. And payback to me because I hurt Jess."

Alice shook her gray head. "I don't believe the good Lord works in payback. Things just happen for a reason."

But what reason, Victoria wondered. Was she supposed to spend the rest of her life longing for a man she couldn't have?

She felt a pull on her dress and glanced down to see Katrina had climbed from the chair and was tugging on her skirt. "C'mon, Toria, go outside with me. I gotta puppy. Wanta see?"

Victoria smiled at Jess's daughter. "Sure, sweetheart. As soon as I drink my lemonade, we'll go look at your puppy and then Victoria has to go home."

Alice's brows pulled together with disappointment. "Oh surely you don't have to go so soon. Jess will be home after a bit. Why don't you stay and have supper with the four of us?"

A sad little smile touched Victoria's lips. "I don't think that would be a good idea, Alice."

The older woman eyed her sternly. "Wouldn't be good for who? You or Jess?"

Chapter Eleven

Jess pulled his vehicle to a stop beside the dark green sedan parked near the front yard gate. The car looked vaguely familiar, but since he'd come home to New Mexico, he couldn't remember seeing it here on the ranch. And then he saw Victoria walking out the front door with Katrina in her arms.

His daughter's arms were tightly wound around Victoria's neck and their cheeks were pressed together. The sight of their closeness didn't surprise him. Back on the T Bar K he'd seen for himself how much Katrina adored Victoria. What did shock him was the idea of Victoria being here on his turf.

Slowly, he left his truck and walked up to the house. By then Victoria had spotted him and set Katrina down on the ground. His daughter ran straight to him, while Victoria lingered on the front porch.

"Daddy! Daddy! Toria's here. See!" She pointed in Victoria's direction.

Jess lifted his daughter into his arms and gave her a fierce hug before he turned his gaze on the woman on the porch. She was wearing a yellow-flowered dress and the wind was causing the hem to flutter around her shapely calves. Her nearly black hair was tousled in loose shiny waves around her shoulders. He'd never seen a more beautiful woman. That had to be the reason his heart was beating like a drum in his chest.

"Yes, Katrina, I see. Now how's my little sweetheart?" he asked her.

She smacked a sloppy kiss against his cheek. "I wanna ride Pokie, Daddy. Can Toria ride, too?"

"I don't think Victoria came here to ride a horse," he said to his daughter. In fact, he wasn't at all sure why she was here. Especially after their stiff parting three days ago.

He set Katrina down on the ground and the child raced back to Victoria's side. Slowly, Jess followed his daughter and stepped up on the porch.

"Hello, Jess."

Jess's eyes met hers and for a moment all he could think about was taking her in his arms and tasting her lips. But he couldn't do that. Especially now, he thought ruefully.

"Hello, Tori."

Her heart ached as she looked at him. "I hope you don't mind me stopping by to see Katrina."

"Wait here," he said, then reached down and took Katrina by the hand. The child began to whine in protest as he led her away.

Stunned, Victoria watched the two of them disappear into the house. Apparently she'd been wrong, she thought sickly. Now that Katrina was well, he didn't want her around his child. He despised her that much. And Alice had almost persuaded her to stay for supper! What a horrible joke that would have been!

Desperate now to get away, Victoria stepped off the porch and walked quickly toward her car. She had almost reached the front gate, when he called to her.

Turning, she saw Jess striding toward her, his face stern, his jaw set. Katrina was nowhere in sight.

"I told you to wait," he said, obviously annoyed that she hadn't obeyed him.

Victoria bristled. "I know we've had our differences, Jess. But I never dreamed you disliked me this much."

Jess watched angry color bloom in her cheeks and, if possible, the passionate explosion of dark pink made her face even more beautiful.

"What are you talking about?" he asked with a blank innocence that only managed to insult her more.

Victoria stared at him. "You *know* what I'm talking about! Katrina. I came by this evening to see her. But you had to hustle her into the house and get her away from the *bad* woman just as fast as you could."

Disgust suddenly tightened his features and roughened his voice. "You must really think I'm a monster."

"Monster might be too good for you," she said between gritted teeth.

"Look Victoria, I realize you and Katrina became close while we were at the T Bar K. And you're wrong. I don't mind you spending time with her. Like you said, she needs female companionship."

Emotion balled in her throat. Swallowing, she turned her head away from him. "I love Katrina," she said quietly. "I guess that's hard for you to understand."

He stared at her and wondered why he felt so helpless and angry that things had went so wrong between them. "What's hard for me to understand is that you could care that much for a child of mine."

Outraged, Victoria's head jerked back around to his and, as her gaze ripped over him, her hands clenched tightly at her sides.

"You've always been blind, Jess Hastings! So blind that you didn't have any idea I could have been raising *your* child these past few years!"

Long moments passed as he stared at her in stunned confusion. Then his eyes turned steely and his jaw tightened to an unyielding ridge.

Closing a hand around her upper arm, he clipped, "Come with me."

Her heart pounded with dread as he led her around to the back of the house where a huge gnarled juniper shaded several wooden lawn chairs.

"What are we doing back here?" she demanded.

He answered in a voice so smooth it chilled her blood. "I thought we ought to have a little privacy while you explain what you just said."

Victoria could feel all the blood draining out of her head and knew her face had turned as white as paper. The ground felt as if it was tilting beneath her feet and for one horrible second, she thought she was going to faint. Dear Lord, why had she opened her mouth like that, she wondered wildly.

Turning her back to him, she prayed for her heart

to slow its frantic pace. "There's nothing to explain, Jess."

His fingers pressed into the flesh of her arm and dared her to look him in the eye. "Don't lie to me, Tori."

Her gaze froze on a limb of the juniper as her mind leaped here and there for a logical reason to give him. But her senses were so scattered she couldn't think, much less come up with an excuse for her loose tongue.

"I was speaking in general terms, Jess. I just meant that if you and I had stayed together—we—we could have had a child."

"No," he said, his voice soft and dangerous. "You weren't generalizing. You flung each and every word at me like a pointed dagger. Now tell me. What did all of that mean?"

Shaking her head, she dared to glance at him. "It doesn't matter," she whispered raggedly.

His hands suddenly gripped her shoulders. "If I thought it didn't matter, I wouldn't be asking. And I'm not going to let you go until you explain yourself."

"Jess, please—"

"Even if it means we stand here all night."

He wouldn't back down, she thought sickly. He was too bullheaded and determined to get what he wanted. Especially now that he was convinced she was hiding something from him.

With a defeated sigh, she turned to face him. "All right, Jess, you want to know, so I'll tell you. Two months after you left for Texas, I learned I was pregnant."

Stunned and in total disbelief, Jess stared at her. "Pregnant!" he repeated as though he never expected to hear her say such a word. "So—where's the child? Our child?"

Closing her eyes, Victoria grimaced as painful memories gripped her with an awful emptiness. "I didn't give birth. I suffered a miscarriage in the fourth month of pregnancy," she said dully.

He didn't say anything and Victoria opened her eyes to see all sorts of emotions flickering across his face, shadowing his gray eyes. In the past four years they'd been apart, she'd often imagined telling him about their lost child. There had been times that she'd longed to tell him. Just to see if he would express the same crushing grief that she had suffered, just to see if he might care the least little bit. But somehow she'd never gotten the chance until now.

When it became obvious he wasn't going to speak, she decided she had to or she was going to break apart from the ache in her chest.

"I didn't tell anyone about the baby," she said, her voice trembling with the need for him to understand. "Not even my family. The only person who knew I was pregnant was the doctor who attended me after the miscarriage."

Anguish twisted his features as he suddenly dropped his hold on her shoulders and turned his back to her. When he finally spoke, his voice dripped with accusation. "Four years! When were you going to tell me? Never?"

Maybe she had been wrong to keep her pregnancy and miscarriage from him, she thought. But that didn't mean he had the right to rake her over the coals. Not after the devastation he'd put her through!

Victoria opened her mouth to defend herself, but before she could utter a word, Jess whirled back around and his eyes were furious as they raked her white face.

"That was *my* child, too!" he practically shouted. "Why did you keep it a secret from me? From everyone? Were you that ashamed to be carrying my baby?"

Tears pooled in her eyes and trickled onto her cheeks. "I wasn't ashamed! I was proud! Thrilled that even though you were gone, I still had a part of you."

Mockery twisted his lips. "Yeah, it really sounds like it."

Ripped by the condemnation in his eyes, she stepped forward and wrapped her fingers around his forearm. "If you'll stop being angry for a moment and listen, maybe you'll understand," she pleaded. "I loved you desperately back then. But I didn't want you to return just because of the baby. I wanted you to come back to San Juan County for *me*." She paused to swallow as emotion threatened to choke her. "I was waiting, hoping and praying that you would come home before my pregnancy grew advanced enough to show. But then the miscarriage happened and it didn't seem to matter—our child was gone."

Dark pain filled his eyes. "But it did matter!" he muttered roughly. "It *does* matter!"

Her head swung sadly back and forth. "Lay all the blame on me if you must. But just so you know, I was making plans to get in touch with you to tell you about the pregnancy when I got the news that you were married. Can't you see how I felt? You had a new wife. You obviously didn't want me in your life and I didn't want to interfere in yours. And then the miscarriage happened and telling you didn't seem all that important anymore.''

Pain such as Jess had never felt before blindsided him. Not until the barbed wire on the pasture fence stuck him in the chest did he realize he'd turned away from Victoria and started walking.

The physical sting jerked him back to reality and he cursed loudly. At the fence, at himself, and the cruel loss of it all.

Across the yard, Victoria watched his fist close around the top wire of the fence, watched as his head bent and his shoulders sagged as though she'd just handed him a load too heavy to carry. In all the years that she'd known him, she'd never seen him react to anything like this. And it shocked her to think he was so devastated to learn of their lost child. What could it mean? Would he have loved their baby as much as he loved his little Katrina?

The notion squeezed her heart and filled her with a desperate need to comfort him. Walking across the yard, she came up behind him and placed her hand on his back.

''I'm sorry, Jess,'' she whispered. ''Truly sorry.''

Slowly his head turned and her heart winced at the loss and confusion she saw in his eyes.

''Why did it happen?''

''The miscarriage?''

He nodded grimly. ''Weren't you taking care of yourself? As a doctor—''

''Of course I was taking care of myself! It was just

one of those things that can't be medically explained. I suppose a higher source decided that it wasn't time for you and I to have a baby together.''

His head bent as a long breath drained out of him. ''If I'd been here it might not have happened.''

Victoria shook her head. ''No, Jess. Your being here wouldn't have changed anything.''

Jess wanted to throw his head back and shout at the unfairness of it all. He and Victoria had lost so much. Not just each other, but a child, too. His decision to go to Texas had done all that.

Suddenly guilt was pouring over him, filling him with a dark weight. He'd made such a mess of their lives. Far worse than he'd known. And for what, he wondered bitterly. His pride? He'd hated the idea of being one of Tucker's cowhands, but looking back on it now, that job would have been a hell of a lot better than losing Victoria and their child.

He never thought he would ever admit such a thing to himself. But he'd just been slapped with the truth and the jolt had shattered him.

''You're probably saying that to make me feel better,'' he mumbled.

''No, I'm saying that because it's the truth. You couldn't have done anything to prevent it. And there wasn't any damage. I can get pregnant again.''

When Jess had first walked up on the porch he'd wanted to kiss her, but now as he took in her solemn green eyes and sad face, he simply wanted to pull her into his arms and hold her close, feel the reassuring beat of her heart against his. If that meant he loved her, he couldn't help it.

His features softened. "I...wasn't thinking the other night when we...could you be pregnant now?"

In spite of their strained relationship, Victoria wished there was a possibility she could be pregnant. To be given another chance to have Jess's child would be a precious gift. But the appearance of her monthly cycle had doused that hope. "You don't have to worry about that," she assured him.

He didn't say anything for a few moments and then his hand lifted and he brushed his knuckles gently against her cheek.

"I could think of worse things happening to me, Tori."

His reply took her by surprise. So did the gentle shadows in his gray eyes. But just as she was wondering what it all could mean, he turned and walked a few steps away from her.

Bewildered by the abrupt change in him, she stared at the back of his broad shoulders. Then after a moment of indecision she went to stand in front of him. "Jess, why did you hustle Katrina into the house?"

"Not for the reason you think." He lifted his head to look at her and wondered how much worse things could get. "And if you'd not leaped to conclusions, you would have heard my explanation. I had something to talk to you about and I didn't want Katrina overhearing anything or being a distraction."

Even though the evening was comfortably warm, the grim expression on his face caused icy chills to run down her spine. There was something else on his mind besides everything she'd just told him about the baby. "What's wrong, Jess? Why are you looking at me like the world is about to come to an end?"

Deciding there wasn't anyway to soften it, Jess didn't hesitate. "We received the coroner's report back from Albuquerque this afternoon and the news isn't good."

She went still, her senses alert. "What do you mean 'not good'? Do they know the identity of the person?"

Jess shook his head. "Unfortunately, no. He's still a John Doe. The case is going to require a lot more investigating before we uncover his identity."

Her eyes widened as she caught his last words. "He? Then you know the remains were that of a man?"

"A man. White and somewhere around the age of sixty-five."

Clearly confused, Victoria made a palms-up gesture. "Well, as far as I'm concerned that should be good news. At least you know a bit more than you did before."

Taking her by the elbow, he led her over to the shade of the juniper and urged her to take a seat in one of the lawn chairs.

Jess pulled a chair up closely in front of Victoria's and took a seat himself. Resting his elbows on his knees, he leaned toward her. "We know more than that, Victoria. The coroner discovered a bullet hole in the victim's skull. The case has been declared a homicide.

Her mouth fell open. Her head swung back and forth in denial. "No, Jess! Oh no! That can't be true!"

"I'm sorry, Victoria. But someone—a man—was murdered on the T Bar K."

Devastated by the news, she stared at him. His suspicions about the body had been right all along, she thought sickly. Jess hadn't been throwing ungrounded accusations at her just as a way to get back at her family.

"How can that be, Jess? Murder seldom happens in San Juan County! And certainly not on the T Bar K!"

"I don't have any answers yet," he said flatly. "But I will get them. I can promise you that."

Fear, wrapped in myriad questions, swirled wildly through Victoria. Once Jess started digging into this evil act, there was no telling what he might uncover, or who might try to stop him. And how was this going to affect her family and the survival of the ranch?

Suddenly shaking, she leaned forward and reached for his hand. Gripping his strong fingers for support, she said, "Jess, this is…scary. Murder isn't some petty misdemeanor. For all we know the murderer could be close by! If you start uncovering the truth, he might come after you!"

Was she really concerned about him, he wondered. Or was she worried his digging would uncover that someone in the Ketchum family was involved in John Doe's death? He despised himself for even asking himself such a thing. More than anything he wanted to believe her concern was all for him. But now that the case had turned into a homicide, there was too much at stake with his job, and his heart, to simply trust her.

"Give me some credit, Victoria. I am a professional lawman. I know better than to take unnecessary risks. Is it me that you're really worried about? Or maybe you're more worried about your family being involved in this."

Victoria couldn't believe what she was hearing. Especially after what she'd just shared with him about their lost baby. But then she should have known that nothing could soften Jess for very long. Especially where she was concerned.

Her features stiff, she pulled away from him and rose to her feet. Lifting her head with pride, she said quietly, "No one in my family is a killer, Jess. But I understand that you have a job to do and you can't leave any stone unturned. I just hope while you're looking that—you'll be careful."

As Jess watched her walk away, he wondered which part of her words he wanted to believe the most.

Chapter Twelve

The next morning, Jess called Deputy Redwing into his office to discuss the John Doe case and only a few minutes had passed before both men realized they had no concrete evidence and very few, if any, clues to work with.

"I think we should back up here a minute," Daniel said from his seat in front of Jess's desk. "We're not exactly sure the murder took place on the ranch. The body could have been dumped there."

"Could have been." Jess drummed his fingers on the arm of his chair. "If the body had been discovered weeks ago, forensics could have told us so much more. For instance, blood splatters, drag marks, horse tracks. As it is—"

"Horse tracks?" Redwing quickly interrupted. "My mind wasn't working in that direction. You think someone might have carried the body to that remote area on horseback?''

Jess rolled his shoulders in an attempt to relieve the kink in the back of his neck. He didn't know it was possible to be this bone weary. If he totaled up all the sleep he'd gotten in the past three nights, he doubted it would equal eight hours. This T Bar K case was going to be a difficult one. But that wasn't the reason he'd been lying awake staring at the dark walls of his bedroom for hours on end. Victoria was consuming his thoughts to the point where he could hardly focus on anything, much less a homicide case.

"Possibly," Jess answered his deputy's question. "It's a cinch the country back on that part of the T Bar K is damn rough. A four-wheel drive vehicle with a high ground clearance can reach it, but a horse is easier going."

Daniel nodded with the same conclusion. "Or a four-wheeler. That's how the medical examiner took the body out."

Leaning up in his chair, Jess rested his elbows on a patch of desk that wasn't piled with papers. "That's true. But I seriously doubt that any of the hands on the T Bar K has ever tried to drive a vehicle to that range of the ranch. It's simply too rough. I doubt anyone has ever tried it."

Redwing arched a brow at him. "Even a killer who is desperate to dump a body?"

Picking up a pen, Jess began to scratch down several words on a notepad. "Even a killer," Jess answered.

"So what are you trying to tell me?" Daniel asked curiously.

"I think whoever took John Doe back to that arroyo knows the country well. He rode back there with intentions of killing the man. Or he'd already killed him and hauled his body out there on horseback."

Daniel folded his arms against his chest as he digested Jess's scenario of what might have happened. "Sounds logical. Except it would take a mighty eventempered horse to carry a dead man."

Jess grinned, appreciating the fast mind of his deputy. "That's right, it would be hard to find a horse willing to carry a corpse. So it stands to reason the two men probably rode out there together. Both alive. Both on horseback. And then for some reason, one shot the other in the head."

"Did the coroner's report state what caliber of weapon was used?"

Jess shook his head. "Not specifically. Only that it was a small caliber. I wouldn't be at all surprised if the weapon doesn't turn out to be a simple .22 pistol. A man out riding the range often carries one."

"So what does that tell us, if anything?" Daniel looked to his boss for answers.

Jess rose from the chair and walked over to the one dusty window in the office. From this vantage point he could see a part of the parking lot and the back end of a building that housed a law firm's offices. Above the rooftop in the far distance were the mountains and the T Bar K. It was incredible how much he missed that place. Missed being there with Victoria.

Clearing away the sudden thickness in his throat, he said, "Not a whole lot. Except that the killer had to be at close range when he fired the shot."

"Do you think the body was thrown into the arroyo? Or had these men already ridden down in it when the murder took place?''

Jess rubbed a restless hand over his hair. It was a hell of a task to keep his thoughts on such hideous happenings, when the only thing his mind wanted to do was think about Victoria.

He still hadn't gotten over the fact that she'd been pregnant with his child. *His child!* How different things might have been if he'd known. Certainly he would have never married Regina. He would have come home to San Juan County, made Victoria his wife and said to hell with Tucker Ketchum. That's what he should have done anyway. Baby or no baby. Jess could see that now. But now was too late. Or was it? He'd been asking himself that question for the past two days, but so far his heart had been too scared to answer.

Forcing his mind back on Daniel's question, he said, ''The body didn't have any broken bones. So it's doubtful he was tossed off the ledge of the arroyo. I figure the shooting took place down in the bottom of the gorge. That way no cowhand riding fence line or hunting a stray calf would happen to see the deed.''

Worried over the preoccupied look on Jess's face, the deputy asked, ''Do you think someone on the T Bar K did the killing?''

''I don't know.''

Daniel grimaced at the automatic answer. ''I'd like to hear your opinion.''

Turning away from the window, Jess returned to his desk. Once he was seated, he scribbled several more words on the notepad. One of which was T Bar K. Next to the ranch's name he wrote Tucker Ketchum. Below the old man's name, he drew the ranch's brand. A capital T over a bar with a capital K underneath.

"If Tucker Ketchum was alive, I'd say hell yes,'' Jess answered. "But Pa tells me the old man has been dead for a little more than a year now. And from what the coroner tells us, our John Doe has only been dead a few weeks.''

"Ross is still there. And he's plenty hotheaded,'' Daniel was quick to point out.

It would crush Victoria if it turned out that her brother was a killer, Jess thought. If he had to arrest the man, she would hate him for the rest of his life. Any chance for them to make a future together would be over. Or maybe he needed to face the fact that his chance with Victoria was over already, he thought ruefully.

"Being hotheaded doesn't make anyone a murderer,'' Jess replied. "And as far as I know, Ross is still out of town on some kind of business trip. As soon as he returns, I plan to have another talk with him.''

"I wonder if they've let the older brother know about all this,'' Daniel mused aloud. "The one that's a Texas Ranger.''

"Seth? I imagine Victoria's talked to him. I think she's always kept her older brother abreast of what's going on in the family.'' Jess tossed down the pen. "You can bet if things get sticky for the Ketchums, Seth will show up.''

The deputy shifted in his seat. "Look, so far we've been going under the assumption that the killer is a man. It could be a woman.''

Jess cast him a wry look. "You think Victoria or Maggie is suspect?"

A sheepish blush crept up the other man's neck. "No! But I think it would be foolish of us to rule out the possibility that a woman might have committed the crime. A female can pull the trigger on a gun just as easily as a male. And some of them can be damned vindictive."

Didn't he know it, Jess thought. Before she'd died, Regina had done everything she could think of to make his life miserable. Including snatching Katrina from day care, when she'd had no parental rights to their daughter.

"I'm not ruling anything out. Especially not the gender of the killer," Jess said rather sharply. "All we've done so far is to make a lot of suppositions."

"We've got to start somewhere. And without the identity of the victim, we don't have much."

Reaching once again for the pen and notepad, Jess underlined the T Bar K brand. "Forensics is working on John Doe's identity. While we wait for a break in that direction, you and I are going to interview the remaining cowboys on the ranch. Then we're going to go over all of our notes with a fine-tooth comb."

Sensing that the discussion was nearing its end, Daniel rose to his feet. "What about Maggie? I still haven't spoken with her."

Jess arched a brow at him. "Anxious to speak with the widow, are you?"

Shrugging, Daniel moved to the corner of Jess's desk. "She's a beautiful woman."

"She's also still grieving over the loss of her husband."

The younger man's closed expression changed to a look of surprise. "Still? It's been a few years since Hugh was killed by that bull."

Jess studied him thoughtfully as his mind automatically turned to Victoria. "Some people never get over losing a spouse or sweetheart. I suspect Maggie is one of them."

"Like you?"

Like him, Jess answered silently. He might as well face the truth. He'd never gotten over losing Victoria. He never would. The only thing left for him to do was learn to live with the pain. Or try to win her back. But how the hell did he expect to do that when he'd gone out of his way to make her hate him?

You could tell her how you really feel, Jess. That you love her. That you've always loved her.

Shaken by the little voice in his head, Jess wiped a hand over his face. "Look, Daniel, I was divorced from Regina when she died in a car wreck. I was terribly saddened by her death. No one wants to see a life snuffed out at an early age. Especially someone you've been close to. But I've been over Regina's death for a long time now."

The deputy eyed him closely. "I'm not talking about your ex-wife. I'm talking about Victoria. She's the one you're carrying a torch for."

Dear Lord, it was a torch all right. Even now, thoughts of the two of them making love were hot enough to scorch him with uncomfortable heat and remind him of how much he wanted her, had always wanted her.

Deliberately avoiding Redwing's last comment, he

handed a copy of the coroner's report to his most trusted deputy.

"Here," he told him. "Study that and then you can drive out to the T Bar K and interview the Ketchum widow."

"Anything specific you want me to ask her?"

Jess settled back in his chair. "All I ask is that you go easy with her."

Clearly offended, Daniel frowned at him. "What did you think I was going to do, throw a pack of cigarettes down on the table and shine a bright light in her eyes?"

Jess tried his best not to smile. "Just don't badger the woman, Redwing. For information or a date."

Starting toward the door, Daniel tossed over his shoulder, "Hey, I can see how miserable you are. I'm not about to start squiring a woman around on my arm. Even one as pretty as Maggie Ketchum."

Victoria rarely went outside the clinic for lunch, but the day was hot and sunny and the four walls of her office were closing in on her. The morning had seen the waiting room spilling over with patients, yet in spite of the heavy load of work, Victoria had overhead Lois and Nevada discussing the murder case, not once, but three times.

Murder on the T Bar K! Even though the news had hit the local and state newspapers, it was still an idea she couldn't quite fathom. Questions about the whole thing continued to pester her head as she walked down the street to a favorite, nearby café.

If the unknown dead man had been killed on their family property, who was he and why had he and the killer been on the ranch in the first place? she wondered. And if the murder had occurred somewhere else, why had the body been dumped in that particular arroyo? To Victoria, the whole idea was not only mind-boggling, it was also terrifying.

Three nights ago, after Jess had told her about the medical examiner's report, she'd called Ross in hopes he'd drop the cattle convention he was attending and hurry home. But upon hearing the news, her brother hadn't expressed that much shock. Nor did he seem overly concerned that a murder investigation was taking place on the T Bar K. Which shouldn't have surprised her. Nothing shook Ross.

But the whole thing had shaken her and eventually she'd decided to make another call to their older brother's home in Texas. Unfortunately, Seth's answering machine had informed her that he would be out for an indefinite period of time. Which meant he was working some case away from San Antonio.

Being a Texas Ranger, Seth would know exactly what to do about this mess, she thought with desperate longing. Victoria was simply a physician who tried her best to keep people alive and well. She didn't know anything about murder cases or how to protect her family from the ramifications of one.

Inside the busy café, Victoria found a seat at the long counter and quickly plucked a menu from its home between a napkin holder and a pair of salt and pepper shakers.

As Victoria's gaze traveled down the listed items for lunch, male voices, coming from somewhere behind her, immediately caught her attention.

"—always knew old Tucker was a shady dealer. Now it looks like things have caught up with him."

Cringing inwardly, her gaze remained fixed on the menu as she debated whether to turn and face the man attacking her dead father or to wait and listen for what else might be said.

Before she could decide, a different voice spoke up which was clearly male and just as insulting as the first one had been.

"Damn right, Porter. And it's about time those Ketchums get brought down from their high horses. When an operation gets as big as the T Bar K, you just about know all that money isn't coming in from cattle sales. There's no telling what Ross is into. Money laundering, probably. If you ask me, he's just a carbon copy of his old man. He wouldn't think twice about shutting someone up with a bullet to the head."

"But nobody's asking you, Jay. So I'd advise you to keep your mouth shut. Unless you want to be sued for harassment."

That was Jess talking!

Victoria's heart leaped as his hand settled warmly over her shoulder. Turning slowly, she gave him a strained smile.

"Hello, Jess."

He squeezed her shoulder in acknowledgement before he turned to face the two gossiping men. Victoria could see the pair were sitting in a booth directly across from her barstool. It was no wonder she'd heard every word they were saying.

In a steely drawl, Jess said to the two men, "I guess you two didn't see Ms. Ketchum walk in and sit down.

Maybe you'd like to take this opportunity to apologize to her. Especially you, Jay.''

Victoria's troubled gaze wavered wildly back and forth between Jess and the two men. The one called Jay appeared to be in his forties with a slab of excess weight around his middle and a lack of hair on top of his head. The other man, Porter, was younger and blond. His fearful expression told Victoria he'd had dealings with Jess before and he wasn't looking forward to having any now.

"Well, well. Now isn't this something." The one called Jay sneered. "San Juan County's big, bad undersheriff cozying up to a Ketchum. Guess we won't have to wonder how this murder investigation is going to turn out."

Anticipating his reaction, Victoria grabbed Jess's arm at the same time he made a lunge toward Jay. "Jess, don't," she pleaded in a low voice. "It isn't worth it."

By now the entire café was watching the scene taking place, but Jess seemed not to care. "Get out of here," he ordered the two men. "You're breathing up too much oxygen for my liking! And if I hear either one of you lipping off again, I'm going to personally have Ms. Ketchum file charges against you."

To her relief, both men got up and silently left the café. Even so, when Jess turned back to her, she was outwardly trembling in the aftermath of what had just taken place.

Grimacing at the sight of her white face, he took her by the arm. "Come on," he said gently, "let's go back here."

She let him lead her through the maze of midday

diners, all of whom seemed more interested in the sight of them together than the food on their plates.

At the back of the room, he helped her into a quiet booth. The two of them were hardly settled in their seats before they glanced up to see a waitress hovering over the table. From the apologetic look on her face, she'd witnessed the unpleasant scene along with the rest of the diners.

"What can I get you two to drink? Something cool?" she asked, glancing pointedly at Jess.

"No, ma'am. You might as well bring me coffee so I can get good and warmed up."

The waitress giggled and Victoria rolled her eyes and smiled in spite of herself. "I'll take coffee, too," she told the blonde.

After the young woman was out of earshot, Jess said, "I'm sorry about that, Victoria. Sheriff Perez issued a statement to the paper about the murder earlier in the week. Now that the news is out, everyone is talking. But Jay is a loudmouth and he obviously didn't know who you were. Just goes to show you he doesn't know your family either."

The fact that he was being so gallant caught Victoria off guard. Normally he'd jump at the chance to bad-mouth the Ketchums. Instead he'd just defended her and her brother and she couldn't imagine why.

"I have a feeling Jay's the sort that would have said all those things whether I'd been sitting there or not," Victoria told him. "But thank you for sticking up for me."

One corner of his mouth lifted into a wry grin. "It's my job to defend innocent ladies."

Her brows arched with a measure of mockery. "Innocent? You mean you don't believe I'm the killer?"

He scowled at her. "No. I don't think you are, or could ever be, a killer. You know that."

Heaving out a heavy breath, Victoria ran a helpless hand through her loose, dark hair. "Oh Jess, this is a nightmare. It's all I hear at the clinic. And what those guys were saying a few minutes ago is probably just a drop in the bucket to what's being said around the county, and the state for that matter." She lifted sad eyes to his face. "Until a few moments ago, I didn't realize my family was so hated. Although, I should have had some clues. You tried to tell me—especially about Daddy."

At one time Jess believed he'd wanted to see the look of anguish on Victoria's face. At one time he'd blamed all his miseries on Tucker Ketchum and the Ketchum family. But in these past few days, he was beginning to see how narrow-minded that thinking had been. He wanted to forget and move forward. Question was, would Victoria want to move forward with him?

"Your family isn't hated, Victoria."

Disbelief widened her eyes. "You heard those men, Jess! If that wasn't hate, what was it?"

"Envy and ignorance. Your family has been a strong focal point in this county for years. Let's face it, your old man had clout. He could pull strings with his political friends in the state capital. A lot of people around here resented that. Especially the local politicians. They don't like anyone going over their heads. Besides all that, you're rich. That always makes tongues wag in the wrong direction."

She studied his rugged face, and as she did her conversation with Alice slipped into her thoughts. From the time he'd been a small boy, Jess had lived in the shadows of an alcoholic father and a mother who'd deserted him. It amazed her that he'd grown up so strong and true to his convictions as a lawman and a father. She admired his strength. Yet she had to admit she also feared it. Because she knew Jess wouldn't stop until he had the culprit of this murder behind bars or dead. Whichever came first.

"Does that mean you believe my family isn't involved in the murder?"

"I don't—" he stopped abruptly as the waitress suddenly appeared at their table and plunked down two mugs of steaming coffee.

The weary blonde looked from Victoria to Jess as though she needed to remind them they were here to eat. "Ready to order now?"

Once Jess had showed up in the café, Victoria had forgotten all about studying the menu. But then Jess had always had the ability to scatter her senses. "Just give me the special," Victoria told her.

"Make that two," Jess added.

The waitress scribbled down their order, then moved on to another table. Victoria arched a brow at Jess.

"You were saying," she prompted.

He glanced around to make sure no one was listening to their conversation. "I don't know who's involved, Victoria. I just hope, especially for your sake, that any of the Ketchums or your employees on the ranch aren't involved."

Leaning toward him, she lowered her voice. "You're talking like a lawman, Jess."

His eyes slowly searched hers, then dropped to settle on her moist lips. "I *am* a lawman, Tori."

She swallowed as heat traveled from the center of her body outward to her arms and legs. "Yes, but I want you to talk to me like a—"

"Lover?" he finished wryly.

Yes! She wanted him to tear open his heart, to expose what he was really thinking. Not just about the murder case, but about his feelings for her, too. But maybe he'd already done that, she thought with defeat. Maybe she needed to realize he didn't *have* any feelings for her. At least, not the special kind.

Tilting up her chin, she asked, "Isn't that what we are—were?"

He stared at her for a long time as he tried to decide if now was the time for him to lay his cards on the table, to tell her that he needed her. No, this wasn't the place for it, he thought. He wanted to be able to say all the things he needed to say without being interrupted.

"We, uh, were a lot of things. Once," he said carefully. "But I—"

"Damn it, Jess!" she hissed under her breath. "I wish you'd quit talking in the past! That's all over with! This is now."

His gray eyes slid back to hers and narrowed with a look of warning. The last thing he wanted now was to argue with her. "I didn't come in here for this, Victoria."

Drawing in a bracing breath, she straightened her shoulders. "What did you come in here for? This is one of my favorite eating places. I don't ever see you in here. Were you following me?''

To her surprise a blush crept up from the collar of his khaki shirt and spread across his square jaw.

''Not exactly.'' But he had been, Jess thought guiltily. He'd seen her walking down the sidewalk, her straight white skirt molded to her curvy bottom, her nearly black hair pinned into a messy twist atop her head. She didn't have to work at looking sexy. She *was* sexy and the sight of her had turned him into a hound dog trailing after the luscious scent of a rabbit. Now he had to admit, even if it was only to himself, that she was the reason he'd decided to forgo a sandwich at his desk.

''I happened to be driving down the street and saw you walk in here. So I figured it would be a good chance to talk to you.'' And it was true that he'd wanted to speak with her today, he thought. But he'd planned to simply call her at the clinic once he figured her patient load was winding down. Seeing her on the street had quickly changed that plan.

Victoria studied him skeptically. ''What did you want to talk to me about?''

Anything, he silently answered. Just hearing her voice filled him with ridiculous joy. And ever since she'd walked away from him the other evening on the Hastings ranch, he'd been miserable. The fact that she'd carried his baby and ultimately lost it was still all new to him, still an open wound in his heart. Over the past days, regret over the loss had alternated with the foolish idea he could somehow make it all up to her.

And let her reject you, hurt you all over again.

The inner voice scared him, but it also stiffened his resolve and he leaned back in the booth and sipped from his coffee cup.

"Yes, I'd planned to call you later this evening."

She looked doubtful. "Oh."

"Yeah," he went on as casually as he could, "I wanted to let you know I was going to be coming out to the T Bar K this evening."

"Ross still isn't home."

"Ross wasn't my reason for coming."

Her stomach tightened and her whole body grew hot as she noticed a subtle smolder in his eyes. "Jess—I'm not going to fall in bed with you again! Sex between us is...wonderful. But—"

"Damn it, Victoria, this isn't the place to be talking about sex!" Especially when just hearing her say the word made his body hard.

Even though his voice had been low, Victoria couldn't help but glance toward the front of the café where the bulk of midday diners were sitting. The two of them had already created one scene with Jay the loudmouth. She didn't want to add more fuel to the gossip.

"I agree," she said stiffly. "So can we change the subject, please?"

Before he could reply, the waitress appeared with their plates of meat loaf and accompanying vegetables. Once she'd served them and went on her way, Jess said, "As much as I'd like to make love to you, Tori, that's not why I'd planned to visit the ranch this evening. I'm going to ride out to the arroyo where your cowhands found John Doe's remains. I thought you might like to ride along with me."

Make love. She was so caught up with those two words she almost missed the last. "Did you say ride with you?" she asked, her face a picture of disbelief

His lips suddenly twisted into a goading grin. "You do still know how to ride a horse, don't you?"

Victoria's medical practice kept her too busy to find much time for horseback riding, but she'd hardly forgotten how to keep her feet in the stirrups. "Better than you," she retorted.

"Then you'll join me?"

Still puzzled about his motives for the invitation, she asked, "What are you going to do out there? I thought the medical examiner and his staff had already combed the place."

"They did. But I want to look for myself. Just in case they might have missed something. And you've always been eagle-eyed. Maybe you'll find a clue that will help put this whole thing to rest."

She inwardly smiled at the thought. It would be wonderful to find information that would clear away the cloud of suspicion hanging over her family's head. "I'd like that," she admitted.

Picking up his fork, Jess dug into the food in front of him. "I'll bring my own mount," he told her. "Just have one for yourself saddled and I'll try to be there around six. Is that too early for you? If you have late appointments, I'll wait."

He'd wait? Something was wrong, Victoria thought. Jess wasn't a patient man. And he didn't need her to help him hunt for evidence. So why did he want her to join him on this ride?

It didn't matter, she quickly told herself. He was going to trust her enough to allow her onto the crime

cene. She couldn't pass up such an opportunity. And
besides all that, she loved the man. She wanted to
spend time with him. If that made her a fool, she
couldn't help it.

"Don't worry," she said. "I'll be ready."

Chapter Thirteen

When Victoria arrived home later that evening, she found Marina in the kitchen preparing supper.

Walking over to where the older woman was standing in front of the huge gas range, she curled an arm around the back of her waist and pecked a kiss on her cheek.

"Hello, *chica*. You home a little early."

Victoria peered over the woman's shoulder at the boiling pot of chicken and dumplings. Maybe she could invite Jess to stay and eat supper with her, she thought. After a long horseback ride, he would have to be hungry.

Don't start getting all hopeful again, Victoria. The man just invited you on a horseback ride, not a trip to the wedding altar.

"I didn't linger at the office," she told Marina. "I needed to get home."

Marina turned her head just enough to see Victoria's face. "You still not smilin'. Why you been sad all week? Jess been botherin' you again?"

A mocking smile tilted Victoria's lips. Jess had been *botherin'* her for years. And would keep on *botherin'* her for years to come if something didn't change his way of thinking about women, about her and the mess they'd made of their relationship.

Pulling the clasp from atop her hair, Victoria shook the chocolate black waves until they spilled around her shoulders.

"I had lunch with Jess today," Victoria admitted. "As a matter of fact, he's going to be here in a few minutes."

The cook turned and faced Victoria head-on. "He's gonna hurt you again, *chica.* I feel it in here." Her lips pressed to a grim line, she tapped her ample bosom which was covered with the bib of a white apron. "I like Jess. But you should look at some other man. Not him."

She couldn't look at some other man, Victoria thought. She couldn't eat or sleep, or make love with another man. Jess had taken up residence in her heart a long time ago. There wasn't room for anyone else.

Her gaze dropped to her feet as hopelessness weighed on her shoulders. "He's not coming here to woo me, Marina. He's coming on business. I'm going to ride with him out to the mesa where the hands found the body."

A horrified expression swept over Marina's face. "No, *chica!* You and Jess mustn't go out there! That place—it's bad. Really bad. Someone will be hurt again. Or killed!"

Marina's desperate outburst took Victoria by complete surprise. It wasn't like the woman to be superstitious about anything.

"How could you know that, Marina? I'm sure you've never even seen the place."

The old woman shook her head vehemently. "I see it in my dreams. That is enough."

In an effort to console her, Victoria smiled and patted her arm. "Oh, Marina, you're getting carried away over nothing. Dreams, even scary ones, are just pictures from our subconscious mind. Just because you dreamed the place was dangerous doesn't mean it's evil ground."

Marina rolled her dark eyes and shook her head. "Death happened there. And evil *is* still there, *chica.* Don't go there," she warned again.

"Marina, this isn't like you at all. You're getting the creeps over nothing. Jess and I are only going out there to look the place over and see if we can find anything to help uncover the truth of what happened. That's all. And once we're finished we'll be back to eat. That is, if I can talk him into staying for supper."

The other woman was clearly disturbed about the whole idea, but finally she sniffed and turned back to the gas range. "Thank goodness your brother is home," she mumbled.

Surprise had Victoria glancing sharply at Marina. "Ross is home? Why didn't you tell me? Where is he?"

Marina frowned at her rapid-fire questions. "Someone call and he took off again." She shook her head in disapproval. "He needs to be here now. Not runnin' to see a bull or a horse."

Ross always called Victoria as soon as he returned from a business trip. She couldn't imagine why he'd failed to this time. Especially when she'd made a point of telling him how anxious she was for him to get back to the ranch and deal with the murder case.

"Will he be back home tonight or did he say?" she asked the cook.

"He said he'd be back."

Victoria sighed with relief. "Good. Now I'd better go get ready before Jess gets here."

As Victoria started out of the kitchen, Marina angled her another stern look. "Be very careful out there, *chica*."

Victoria waved a dismissive hand at her warning. "Don't worry, Marina. We'll be fine."

Thirty minutes later, she was dressed in jeans, boots, a pale blue shirt and with a cream-colored Stetson dangling against her back. She watched her cousin, Linc, saddle her favorite mount on the ranch, a spotted mare called Dixie.

"Linc, there's no need for you to be doing that," she gently scolded. "I've been saddling horses since I was eight years old. I can do it."

The tall, brown-haired cowboy smiled over at Victoria and as always, she thought how much he resembled Ross, even though the two men were cousins rather than brothers.

Thirty-two years ago Linc had been born to Randolf and Darla Ketchum, brother and sister-in-law to Tucker. From what Victoria remembered of her uncle Randolf, he'd been the exact opposite of Tucker. Quiet, unassuming and not nearly as ambitious. Years ago he'd been partners with her father in the building of the T Bar K. But when his heart had started to fail, he'd sold his quarter of the place to his brother. Several years later, when Victoria and Linc were in high school, Randolf's heart had finally given out just as Tucker's had.

After Randolf's death, Darla quickly remarried and moved back east to a small city on the coast. As far as Victoria knew, Linc rarely heard from the woman and she often wondered if Darla had resented the fact that Linc had chosen to stay and live with his aunt and uncle on the T Bar K rather than move east with her.

"It's no problem, Victoria," Linc said. "I've already called it quits for the day. Once I finish here I'm going to put up my feet and rest."

Victoria smiled at him. "Good. I know you've had a busy week. What with all the mares foaling now and keeping the remuda ready for roundup, it's a wonder you have time to draw a good breath."

He pulled the saddle cinch tight, then tucked off the loose end of the leather strap. "Spring on the T Bar K is the best time of the year. All the youngins being born and the wildflowers blooming. Makes a fella glad to be alive."

The shuffle of footsteps had them both glancing around at the opposite end of the long shed row. Victoria's heart gave a little leap as she saw Jess striding quickly toward them. He wasn't wearing his badge this evening, she noted, but his .45 was resting in the holster on his hip. The sight of the weapon made her wonder if he was expecting trouble.

Although Linc had finished saddling Dixie, he stood

beside Victoria and waited to greet Jess with a hand-shake before he excused himself. A sign to Victoria that the two men liked and respected each other.

As the head wrangler for the T Bar K walked away, Jess said, "That's one Ketchum I can say I've always liked."

With a wan smile, Victoria gathered up the mare's reins. "I was just thinking how Linc looks like Ross, but his personality is like his father's." She glanced over at Jess. "You would have liked Uncle Randolf if you'd had the chance to know him. He was a quiet, unassertive guy, nothing like Daddy."

"I'll bet Linc was always glad about that," Jess said with a grin.

Victoria's lips pressed together. "If that's the sort of thing I'm going to be hearing from you on this little trip, then I don't think I want to go."

He quickly held up a hand. "All right," he conceded. "I shouldn't have said that. You loved your father and you don't want to hear anyone bad-mouthing him. So I'll try not to do it again."

She looked at him, her expression suddenly regretful. What was wrong with her? Ever since lunch, she'd been looking forward to sharing this evening with him. The last thing she wanted to do was start an argument between them.

Sighing, she said, "I'm sorry, Jess. I guess I'm tired of Daddy being a testy issue between us. I don't want him to stand between us anymore."

Jess didn't want Tucker, their past or this damn murder case to stand between them. Maybe he should take her aside right now and tell her exactly that, he thought. Then just as quickly he pushed the notion out of mind. There wasn't much daylight left and it would take them at least an hour to reach the crime scene. When he did talk to Victoria about the two of them starting over, he didn't want to be rushed. They could always ride back in the dark.

Besides that, Jess needed a little more time to bolster his courage. Even if he confessed to Victoria that he still loved her, it wasn't as if she was going to fall gratefully into his arms. More than likely she wouldn't believe him. After all, he'd gone out of his way to convince her he was incapable of loving her or any woman. He couldn't blame her if she told him that his feelings didn't matter anymore. That he'd hurt her too much to ever trust him again.

Dear Lord, he couldn't think those black thoughts now, he desperately told himself. He had to believe that she still cared enough to give him another chance.

"I don't want him to be an issue between us either," Jess said, and before he could stop himself he stepped forward and cupped his palms against the sides of her face. "I haven't seen you like this in a long time, Tori. You look beautiful this evening."

His hands left her face to smooth down her arms, then settle on her waist. Her heart pounded and her voice was breathy as she said, "You promised you weren't coming out here to the ranch for sex."

Humor creased his face and she marveled at his light mood and the fact that he was touching her. Something she wanted so much. Needed so much.

"I don't remember making any such promise."

She drew in a deep breath through her nostrils and the scent of him mingled with the smell of hay and horses. ''Well, maybe not a promise. But you assured me you were coming out here tonight on business.''

''Is this sex?'' he whispered. Bending his head, he brushed his lips against her cheeks, her chin and nose. ''Is that all this feels like to you?''

Her lashes fluttered down against her cheeks, her hands trembled to touch him. ''Jess, I—''

The remainder of her words halted abruptly as Dixie suddenly tugged on the reins and whinnied loudly in Victoria's ear.

Turning their heads to see what had drawn the mare's attention, they watched as a wrangler leading a big bay horse passed a few feet away from them. Victoria didn't recognize the young man, but that wasn't unusual. Now that she was practicing medicine, she didn't have much time to spend around the ranch yard. Workers came and went without her ever knowing about the changes.

From his open stare, this particular cowboy seemed to find the sight of Jess and Victoria very interesting, but the moment he realized they had spotted him, he turned his attention straight ahead as though he was embarrassed to be caught gawking.

Clearly irritated at the interruption, Jess watched the young man lead the bay to a nearby stall. ''What was he looking at? Hasn't he ever seen a man kissing a woman?''

Shaking her head, she said, ''Jess, you're a lawman. He's probably wondering why you're kissing me instead of handcuffing me.''

''Handcuffing you,'' he repeated inanely. ''For what?''

She rolled her green eyes. ''You've been investigating a murder. That *is* what you're here for, isn't it?''

To her surprise, he caressed her cheek, then took her by the upper arm. ''Come on. It's time we got down to business.''

Leading Dixie behind her, Victoria walked with him to a spot behind the horse barn where he'd parked his truck and trailer. A big gray gelding was already saddled and tied to the back of the rig. As Jess approached, the animal perked his ears and whinnied softly.

''He's beautiful,'' Victoria said of the horse. ''What's his name?''

The compliment filled Jess with pleasure, making him realize how much he'd always wanted Victoria's admiration. ''We call him Chito. Pa raised him from one of our mare's on the ranch.''

''Will is a cowboy through and through. It's no wonder you've always had good horses on the Hastings ranch.''

He walked over and offered Victoria a hand up. Once she was settled in the saddle, he said, ''We have a few good horses. But not like this place. Wasn't it just last year that the T Bar K won an award for best remuda?''

Smiling with pride, she pulled the hat onto her head and drew the stampede string up tight beneath her chin. ''We can thank Linc for that. He understands what it takes to make good, reliable ranch horses.''

Jess tossed the reins over Chito's neck and swung himself up in the saddle. Leather creaked under his weight as he settled his boots in the long stirrups.

He reined the gray in a westerly direction and Victoria's mare fell in step beside the handsome gelding.

"Linc tells me that Ross's stallion is still missing," he said. "It surprises me that the horse hasn't shown up somewhere close by now."

"I know what you mean. It's not like a stallion is something that could easily be hidden. But then I don't believe the horse has been stolen. I think he's just off visiting some wild mares up in the mountains," she told him, then as a new thought struck her, she glanced at him thoughtfully. "Jess, do you think the stallion's disappearance could have something to do with the murder?"

Jess rubbed his chin as he contemplated the idea. "The notion crossed my mind. But right now I'm not seeing the connection. We just don't have enough clues to piece together."

Just ahead of them, the mountains began to peter out and flatten into a wide open mesa covered with juniper, blue sage, tall yucca and grass. Straight in front of them, the sun was a yellow ball in a blue New Mexico sky.

This was the first time in ages that Victoria had been riding and she'd almost forgotten how wonderful it was to be out on the range with powerful horseflesh beneath her and the smell of sage all around her, the sun and wind on her face.

Yet nature's splendors were responsible for only a part of the pleasure she was feeling. Jess was with her, his tall rangy frame loose in the saddle, his rugged face shaded by the brim of his black Stetson. Just having him this close, sharing this evening with her, filled Victoria with a joy and contentment that nothing else could give her.

For the next few minutes they were silent as the horses picked a trail through tender wildflowers and spiky yucca. Eventually Victoria said, "This evening, when I told Marina what you and I were going to do, she just about had a spell."

He glanced over at her, his expression curious. "A spell? What do you mean?"

"She was scared, worried. She says the place where the man was killed is evil ground. She kept saying that you and I shouldn't go there. That something bad might happen to us."

"Hmm. I didn't know Marina was into Native American lore."

Victoria shook her head. "That's just it, Jess. She isn't. That's why it was so surprising when she started giving me such dire warnings and talking about evil ground."

Jess's brows arched beneath the brim of his black hat. "Maybe she knows more about this whole thing than she's telling."

Shocked by the suggestion, Victoria stared at him. "Oh no, Jess! What could Marina know? She rarely ever leaves the ranch yard!"

"She has friends and relatives that could have said things."

"No," Victoria repeated with firm certainty. "Marina is like a second mother to me. Believe me, if she knew anything at all about this, she would tell you. But she is scared, Jess. I think she has the idea that the killing isn't over."

His face grim, Jess looked at her. "She could be right, Tori."

Victoria came close to shivering in her saddle. "Then I hope we find something, Jess. For both our sakes."

Nearly forty minutes later they rode down into a narrow draw. On both sides of the gulch, twisted juniper bushes grew between slabs of red rock and tufts of grass. Chito's and Dixie's shoes clattered against the boulder-strewn bottom, then the sound changed to that of hooves splashing through shallow water.

Eventually the arroyo opened up wider, the walls grew taller and the ground began to climb in steep increments. Washed out spots made the going slow and precarious. Several times they were forced to travel single file. On these occasions Jess continually glanced over his shoulder to make sure Victoria was following safely. At one point, he even took hold of Dixie's bit and led the mare while Victoria held onto the saddle horn with both hands.

When her legs finally began to ache from the strain of riding, she asked, "How much farther, Jess?"

"We're here."

Wondering what could have possibly alerted him to the fact, she looked around her. There was nothing to see but more arroyo, more boulders and scattered holes of shallow water.

"I don't see anything. How do you know this is the spot?"

"I was here when the medical examiner recovered the body. I remembered."

She was astounded. "How could you? This place

is in the middle of nowhere. I thought I'd been all over the ranch before, but I've never been this far back.''

"From what Ross tells me, this is about a mile away from the west boundary line of the T Bar K.''

Interest peaked her brows as she looked in that direction. "Oh. Who owns the neighboring land?''

"You don't know your own neighbors?'' he teased.

"Yes, I know my neighbors,'' she countered sassily. "Just not from this vantage point.''

He smiled. It had been so long since the two of them had simply talked and laughed. Just to have this sort of closeness with her was precious to Jess.

"Okay,'' he said. "I'll take pity on you. To the west is Rube Dawson's place. Remember him?''

Victoria nodded. "Yes, he's lived there for years. In fact, I treated him last month for an injury to his hand. Said he'd busted it up while fixing fence.''

"Is that what the injury looked like to you?''

She shrugged. "There were several puncture wounds typical of those made by barbed wire. But I didn't really question him about how he'd come by the injury. I was more interested in treating his hand and making sure he knew how to take care of it once he was home. Why? You don't think Rube had anything to do with the killing, do you?''

Jess tugged on the brim of his hat while his eyes squinted toward the western horizon. "Not necessarily. But like I told you before, Tori, I have to think of everyone as a suspect.''

Groaning impatiently at his generalized answer, she gestured to the area surrounding them. "I would have

hought there would be yellow crime tape or some-
hing to show where the body was discovered.''

He gave her a droll look as he swung himself out
f the saddle.

"Think about it, Victoria. What good would a piece
f tape do out here? Tell the deer or cows not to step
ast it?''

Dixie chose that moment to bob her head and Jess
huckled.

Victoria smirked a face at him. "No, smarty. It
vould mark the spot for other investigators.''

"The next good rain will send water rushing
hrough this coolie like a freight train. A piece of
rime tape wouldn't last. And anyway, all the inves-
gation done here at the crime scene is finished.''

She shot him a dry look. "Then what are we doing
ut here?''

Walking over to her and the mare, he held up his
rms in an invitation to help her to the ground. Her
eart hammering with anticipation, Victoria slung her
eg over the saddle horn and put her hands on his
houlders. His hands gathered around her waist and
vith no effort at all, plucked her off the mare's back.

Once she was in his arms, he allowed her weight
o slowly lower to the ground. As the front of her body
lid against his chest, their eyes locked and remained
hat way even after her boots were firmly planted a
ew inches from his.

The corners of his mouth tilted upward as his hands
noved temptingly up and down her rib cage. "You're
bout to find out, Tori.''

Chapter Fourteen

"Something is wrong with you, Jess. You're be having strangely. You have been ever since we ha lunch together at the café."

The urge to kiss her, to take her in his arms an cradle her head against his chest gripped him like fierce, relentless hand. But he couldn't give in to th longing just yet. Daylight was fading and they sti had a job to do.

Smiling wanly, he said, "I've never tried to hid the fact that I like to touch you, Tori. What's s strange about me doing it now?"

She cocked her head to one side as she carefull studied his face. "I'm not talking about that. Go knows we've always had trouble keeping our hand off of each other. You just seem different—like yo don't hate me anymore."

The smile disappeared and his face grew serious as he lifted a hand to her cheek. As the tips of his fingers traced patterns over her smooth skin, he said, "I've never hated you, Victoria. I've been angry with you. And disappointed. But I could never hate you."

His touch was driving her crazy, but it was his words that managed to shake the ground beneath her. Could she be crazy to let herself believe his feelings were softening toward her? Hope spurted through her, but she quickly dashed it down. She'd learned the hard way that Jess could be hot as fire one minute and cold as ice the next. This was probably just one of his warm streaks, she told herself. By the time they got back to the ranch, he'd more than likely be reminding her that nothing could ever be between them.

The dismal thought clouded her eyes as she continued to look up at him. "Jess, you—"

"Enough about me," he suddenly interrupted, then catching ahold of her hand, he tugged her away from the spot where they were standing. "Come on. We're burning daylight. Let's tether our horses and have a look around."

They led Chito and Dixie to a couple of nearby juniper bushes. Once the horses were securely tied, Jess motioned for her to follow him.

About twenty yards away from the spot where they'd left their mounts, Jess guided her to a lone pine tree growing at a slant from the edge of the wide wash. At the base of the trunk were slabs of rock which formed a smooth, rather large V-shape in the gravel bed.

Jess pointed to the deep indention. "This is where our men found the body. It had washed up against

the pine trunk and I suppose the rocks kept it fro
moving on down the arroyo.''

Victoria felt sick as she imagined the man's remai
lying in such a desolate spot, vulnerable to wild ar
mals and the elements. ''Then you don't know th
this is exactly where the crime was committed,'' sl
stated the obvious. ''It could have washed to th
spot.''

Jess nodded. ''Redwing is trying to match up tl
local weather reports to the coroner's time of death
see how many heavy rains have occurred since th
time. I can think of only one.''

Victoria looked hopelessly around them. ''Then i
a cinch you didn't find a bullet casing in the area.
probably washed on down into the San Juan and ov
onto the Apache reservation!''

''We haven't found any yet. Something that sma
probably settled in with the gravel. Let's walk
stream and see if we can find anything. For all v
know the weapon could have been left around he
close.''

They began to hike over the boulder-strewn bed
the arroyo and Victoria asked skeptically, ''Jess, wh
kind of killer would be so stupid to leave the murd
weapon behind?''

He grunted with amusement. ''Most criminals a
very stupid, Victoria. That's why they get caught.''

She glanced hopefully over at him. ''Do you thi
you'll catch this one?''

His gray eyes narrowed with determination. ''Son
cases like this are never solved. But I'm not about
let the book be closed on this one until we have tl

erson or persons who did this thing. And I'm certain
heriff Perez will be just as resolute.''

Her breathing was becoming ragged as their climb
eepened. ''I hope you're right, Jess. If it's not
olved, this thing will be a blight on the ranch and my
amily.''

''You're certain none of your family or T Bar K
ands are involved, aren't you?''

She didn't hesitate. ''Very certain.''

With a worrisome frown creasing his forehead, he
aused to look at her. ''And what will you do if they
re?''

Squaring her shoulders, she said, ''If that time ever
omes, I'll just have to deal with it somehow.''

For the next hour she and Jess combed the bed of
e gulch, looking under loose stones and around veg-
tation for anything that might have been left behind
y a human, but unfortunately they had no luck. Even-
ally, Jess decided they should get their horses and
de up out of the arroyo.

Since the walls of the natural canyon were so steep,
e two of them were forced to search for a spot where
e horses could get a better foothold. The going was
ore than rough and Victoria came close to slipping
ff the back of the saddle when Dixie made a huge,
nal lunge to reach the top.

''Whew! I'm glad that's over with,'' she exclaimed.

From a few feet away, Jess admired the picture she
ade on the spotted mare. Her clothes were dirty and
er hair had loosened from its clasp to tangle about
er shoulders. Pink color stained her cheeks and sweat
as trickling from her temples. Those who knew her

as their family physician wouldn't recognize her, h thought.

But then a lot of the townsfolk probably didn know that Tucker had taught his daughter to ride an work cattle with the best of the men. Because of he upbringing, Victoria had never been a shrinking viole and Jess had to admit he'd always loved her toughnes and determination. In truth, he loved everything abou her. He'd never stopped. And he figured it was pas time to tell her so.

"Getting tired?" he asked.

She slipped the Stetson from her head and wiped hand against her damp forehead. "A little. Are yo ready to head back to the ranch or do you want search some more?"

His expression went serious as he pulled Chito to halt. "Let's get down for a minute. I want to talk t you."

This time Victoria didn't wait for him to help he off the mare. Instead she quickly slid to the groun With the reins in her hands, she started toward Jes At the same time, her toe connected with the root a juniper tree and she stumbled slightly. In the act righting herself, her gaze automatically swept th ground around her boots.

"Oh look, Jess! Here's a piece of leather."

Bending down, she picked up the flat strings leather that were attached together on one end. Eac string was about three-eighths of an inch wide an eighteen or more inches long. She held them up f Jess to see.

Spotting her find, he left Chito and hurried over t her. "Where were these?" he asked with interest.

"Right here," she said, pointing to the ground at er feet. "Where do you think they come from?"

"They're the strings off of someone's saddle. 'hey're used to tie on your bedroll." He gestured to . pair just like them on the back of Victoria's saddle. 'See?"

"Hmm. Do you think they might be significant to he case?"

"Hard to say," he answered thoughtfully. "Some of the T Bar K men could have lost them when they vere back here hunting Ross's stallion."

Her lips pursed to a grim line. "They might have lost saddle strings, but they found a dead man."

Jess stuffed the pieces of leather in his back jeans pocket. "Forget that for right now," he said. "I have something else to talk to you about."

Surprise flickered over her face as his hands came down on her shoulders. "It's going to be getting dusky soon," she pointed out. "Don't you want to wait until we get back to the ranch?"

He shook his head. "No. I've waited too long for this already. I don't want to wait any longer."

"Okay—" she paused as the sound of a rock falling into the arroyo caught her attention. Glancing around his shoulder, she noticed Chito had wandered away and was nipping at a clump of grass growing on the very lip of the canyon.

"Jess! Your horse!"

Whirling around, he cursed as he saw Chito's dangerous position. "Damn horse! He's going to kill himself!"

Oblivious to the miniature landslide his hooves were creating down the side of the gorge, Chito con-

tinued grazing at the sparse tufts of grass. Careful no
to spook him, Jess walked over to the horse.

"Be careful, Jess," Victoria called out to him
"Don't get too close to the edge."

He flashed her a smile as he reached for Chito'
reins. "I'm glad—"

The rest of his words were shattered as a sho
cracked over the mesa, exploding the quietness aroun
them. Victoria watched in wild confusion as Chito
bolted away in a frightened gallop. Jess grabbed at a
spot on his shoulder and then, to her utter horror, tee
tered over backward into the ravine.

"Jess! Oh my God, Jess!"

Not stopping to wonder if the shooter was ready to
take aim at her, too, she looped Dixie's reins over a
nearby pine tree limb and raced toward the spot where
Jess had gone over.

"Oh no! No!" she gasped as she spotted him lying
lifeless at the bottom of the arroyo. He couldn't be
dead! He just couldn't!

Her heart racing with fear, she glanced wildly
around her. She had to get to him! But from this angle,
the walls of the small canyon were so steep she didn't
know if she could make the drop on foot.

For several moments, Victoria ran back and forth
along the lip of the wash to hunt for a better foot trail.
But there was none to be found, so she sat down on
the ledge, swung her legs over and began the descent
by scooting on her bottom.

Halfway down, she heard the sound of a horse's
hooves pounding the ground in a run and nearby brush
popping. She prayed that Dixie hadn't spooked and

tarted for home. With Chito already gone, she needed ome way to ride out of here to get help.

Another thought struck her and she glanced eerily around her and listened for any more sounds out of the ordinary. That could have been the sniper galloping away, she thought frantically. Or maybe the maniac was still around, waiting until she reached Jess before he decided to shoot again.

She mentally slapped herself. She couldn't worry about that now; she had to be brave. All that mattered was that Jess was alive and that she get to him.

The next few minutes Victoria slipped and clawed her way over rocks, roots and damp earth until the ground leveled out. Once she could stand, she stumbled and ran the last few feet to where Jess was lying on his side.

A hand of fear gripped her heart, as she kneeled over him and rapidly searched for a pulse in his neck. Agonizing moments passed before she finally picked up a faint thump-thump beneath her fingertips. The relief that rushed through her was so great, she actually moaned.

His heartbeat was weak, but, thank God, it was here.

"Jess! It's Victoria! Wake up and talk to me!"

When he didn't respond, she quickly turned her attention to his outward condition. Aside from being covered with dirt and mud, a large spot of red was pooling on the shoulder of his denim shirt. Blood was also trickling down from his hairline and onto his forehead. A lesser abrasion ran along one cheekbone and part of his jaw.

Seeing him like this made the woman in her want

to scream and cry. This was the man she loved! But the doctor in her tempered her panic and told her she had to keep her head and help him as best she could.

As gently as possible, she tore open his shirt to inspect his shoulder. Thankfully, the bullet had missed his vital parts and had ripped through a portion of thick muscle and tendon. Although he was leaking quite a bit of blood, she breathed a sigh of relief that no major artery had been torn.

With swift, efficient movements, Victoria removed her shirt and tore off the bottom half to make a compress. For long minutes she applied pressure until she was satisfied the flow of blood was stemmed. After she bound his shoulder with a makeshift bandage, she turned her attention to the wound on his head. Of the two injuries, she feared this one was the worst.

The gunshot to his shoulder was not enough to make him lose consciousness. Apparently during the fall, he'd whacked his head on a rock or something solid. She could only hope the damage wasn't any more than a minor concussion.

"Oh Jess," she whispered as she fought back a flood of tears. "My darling Jess. Just hang on. I can't lose you. Not now. Not ever!"

Tearing another strip of fabric from her shirt, she cleaned the wound on his head and the abrasions on his face as best she could, then sat back on the ground beside him and tried to do some logical thinking.

She had to get him out of here and to medical help. But how? Even if she could get him astride Dixie, he couldn't sit up and make a forty-minute ride back to the ranch!

The only choice she had was to ride out for help.

and hope that while she was gone the sniper didn't decide to come back for a final, fatal shot.

If only she had a cell phone!

The thought jerked her gaze back to Jess's lifeless form. While he'd been staying on the T Bar K, she'd seen him taking a small, flip-cased phone from his shirt pocket. Could he be carrying the phone on him now? More importantly, had the communication piece survived his fall?

She made a dive at his chest and nearly shouted with elation when she unbuttoned one of the pockets on his denim shirt and pulled out the small cell phone.

Holding her breath, she pressed the power button.

Nothing happened.

Furiously, she whacked the instrument against her palm and tried again.

To her amazement, the phone lit up and tears of relief flowed down her cheeks as she punched in the number for emergency help.

Once she'd relayed the problem and directions of how to find them, Victoria asked the man to connect her to the sheriff's office on the slim chance that Deputy Redwing would be there.

God was obviously with her because the deputy came on the line immediately.

"And you say Jess was shot?" he asked after Victoria had relayed her story to him.

The seriousness in his voice only underscored the fear inside Victoria. Her shaking hands nearly dropped the telephone as she cried, "Yes! The bullet hit his shoulder and knocked him over the ledge!"

"Did you see who did the shooting?"

"No. I think the shot came from a southeasterly

direction, but I can't be sure. It all happened so suddenly. The loud explosion, Chito bolting and Jess falling. My eyes were on him—I didn't see anybody anywhere. And afterward, I was more worried about getting down here to Jess.''

''What about now?'' Daniel asked sternly. ''Can you see anything? Hear anything?''

She looked around her and listened intently. Dusk was falling rapidly and in the far distance she could hear a pack of coyotes yipping and howling. She'd never felt so alone or helpless in her life. ''No. It's practically dark now. I can't see much. And the only thing I can hear is the wind whistling through the pines and a pack of coyotes.''

Silent moments passed and Victoria knew the deputy was taking the time to assess the situation in his mind.

''Is Jess carrying his weapon?'' he asked.

Victoria glanced at the holster still fastened around Jess's hips. Somehow the .45 had made the ride down into the gulch with him.

''Yes,'' she answered.

''Do you know how to use it?'' the deputy asked.

Even though he couldn't see her, Victoria nodded. ''Yes. Jess taught me. A long time ago,'' she said around the lump in her throat.

''Good. Then get the revolver and keep it in your hands until we get there.''

''I will,'' she promised. ''Just please hurry! I'm so afraid for Jess.''

Minutes later a rescue helicopter circled once, then twice and finally came to land on a flat shelf of ground above the arroyo. Immediately, a team of paramedics armed with portable equipment started down the steep wall of the wash.

When the four of them reached the spot where she sat close to Jess's side, one of the men said, "We'll take it from here, Miss."

"He needs—"

"We're trained paramedics, Miss. You'll be helping him more by getting out of the way and letting us do our jobs."

Before she could tell them she was a doctor, they were lifting Jess away from her and laying him out on a stretcher.

"Be careful! He has a concussion!" she warned as she pushed her stiff form to her feet.

The paramedics ignored her and she groaned with frustration.

"Don't worry, I'll make sure they let you fly back to the hospital with him."

Victoria whirled toward the deep male voice and found Deputy Redwing standing directly behind her. With a great sigh, she wearily pushed a hand through her disheveled hair.

"Thank you," she said gratefully, then motioned toward the ground several feet above their heads. "Did you notice if my mare is still up there?"

Glad to give her that much good news, he smiled. "She's still tied to the pine. I'll take care of her for you."

"Just take her saddle off and slap her on the rump," Victoria told him. "She'll go back home on her own."

"What about the saddle?"

"Just leave the saddle there under the pine. Some of the hands will come after it later."

As soon as the words were out, she swayed on her feet and the deputy grabbed her arm to steady her.

"Are you okay?" he asked.

Finding an inner strength she didn't know she possessed, Victoria pulled herself together and nodded at the lawman. "I'll be fine. It's Jess that I'm worried about."

Deputy Redwing glanced over to where the paramedics were attaching an IV drip to Jess's arm. "How is he?"

Struggling to keep from breaking down in sobs, she swallowed hard and wiped a hand over her face. "He hasn't regained consciousness since the fall."

Concern plowed furrows in the deputy's forehead. "Why is that? Has he gone into shock?"

As her gaze went back to Jess and the paramedics, she was swamped with helplessness and deep anger. How could someone be so evil as to want to kill Jess?

"No. I don't think so," she answered Redwing's question. "At least, not yet. And now that medications have been started, I don't believe shock will be a problem. It's the trauma to his head. Apparently he whammed it pretty hard."

Releasing his hold on her arm, he said, "He'll wake up, Ms. Ketchum. Jess's head is the hardest part about him."

She tried to smile at his words of encouragement, but her lips felt frozen. Maybe she was going into shock herself. The idea of losing Jess was certainly more than she could bear right now.

"I pray that you're right, Deputy Redwing."

He patted her shoulder. "Do you think you can

climb out of here? They'll be loading Jess in the helicopter soon."

She pulled on her hat and straightened the remnants of her tattered blouse. "Yes, I'll make it. Just don't let them leave without me."

"Has there been any change?"

Victoria glanced up from her vigil at Jess's bedside to see that Ross had entered the hospital room. Last night her brother had been waiting at the emergency room to meet them, but later after they'd gotten Jess settled and stabilized, he'd gone back to the ranch to catch some sleep. She was glad he was back. She'd never felt so lost or alone in her whole life.

"Not that I can tell," she said wearily. "I'm still waiting to hear if Doctor Wallis plans to run another brain scan. The last one didn't show any evidence of damage to his brain. But..." her voice trailed away on a worried note.

Ross came to stand next to his sister, who was sitting in the same plastic chair she'd been in since Jess had been brought into the room.

"The doctor hasn't been around this morning?" he asked.

She grimaced as she glanced from her brother to the faint gray light filtering through the slatted blinds on the window. It was almost daylight. Hours had passed since Jess's lifeless body had been carried out of the arroyo, and though his vital signs were stable, he hadn't lifted one eyelid or made any sound. His continued state of unconsciousness frightened her through and through.

"No. Doctors have a habit of disappearing when you need them the most."

Ross smiled at her dry humor. "I'm sure that's what most of your patients say." He looked down at her weary face. "Speaking of patients, what about your clinic? You can't go in today. You're dead on your feet."

"Even if I were rested, I wouldn't leave Jess. Dr. Martinez will fill in for me."

Her brother leveled a stern look on her. "What you need to be doing is going home to the ranch and going to bed. You've been here all night, Victoria. You've got to get some rest."

Shaking her head, she rose to her feet and walked over to the room's single picture window and turned open the blinds. Staring out at the gray parking lot of the hospital, she said, "I can't leave. Not until I know he's going to be all right."

Ross was about to respond to her argument when the door swished open and a young nurse walked into the room.

"Looks like our patient is still sleeping," she said.

Victoria arched a brow at the name tag pinned to the woman's scrub top. "He's not sleeping, Tanya. He's unconscious."

The nurse glanced at her sharply before she placed a metal clipboard on the nightstand. For the next few minutes the room was quiet as she monitored the drip on Jess's IV, then checked his vital signs and recorded them in the medical chart.

When she started toward the door without a word, Victoria stepped in her path. "Let me see that, please."

The nurse looked incredulous. "What?"

Victoria stretched out her hand. "Jess's chart. Let me see it."

"I'm sorry, but that's against regulations—"

"Hang the regulations! I'm a doctor. An M.D. right here in Aztec!" Victoria practically shouted.

Wide-eyed, the nurse shook her head. "But—but you're not Mr. Hastings's attending physician," she argued.

Victoria was suddenly furious. "I've been waiting here for hours to hear if the neurologist is going to run another scan on Jess's brain. Now you come in here and behave as though his vital signs are supposed to be a secret! Give me—"

The young nurse pressed the clipboard securely against her chest. "Are you a relative of Mr. Hastings?"

"No."

"Then if you're not his physician and you're not a relative, you really don't have a right—"

"Look, I'm Mr. Hastings's—" Victoria paused and her face suddenly flamed as she realized the only word for it was lover. And in Jess's opinion, she wasn't even that much. She was just a sex partner. No more. No less.

Ross quickly moved across the room and stepped between the two women. "Uh, sorry, nurse. My sister is very upset. You see, she's in love with Mr. Hastings. She's concerned about his welfare."

Hearing her feelings for Jess expressed out loud acted like a slap to her runaway nerves. She quickly apologized to the nurse, then walked over to the window where she wearily pressed a hand against her burning eyes. Behind her she could hear Ross doing his best to mollify the indignant nurse.

Once the door swished closed behind the young woman, Ross turned to his sister. "Victoria, what in hell is wrong with you? You know better—"

Her emotions tied in knots, Victoria whirled on him. "Yes, I know better! But you don't understand what this has been like for me, Ross. Someone tried to *kill* Jess! Right on our own property!" Her troubled gaze focused on Jess's silent form. "And now I don't know if Jess is going to live or die. I might not ever hear his voice again. He might—"

"Stop it!" Ross ordered as he pulled her against his broad chest and patted her back. "You've got to get a grip on yourself, sis. If you keep going at this rate, you're going to have a mental breakdown."

Victoria shuddered as she tried to get control of her scattered nerves. "Oh Ross, this whole thing with the murder is so unbelievable. And then to see Jess shot before my very eyes!"

"Damn it, Victoria, why did you two go out there anyway?"

Rearing her head back, she gazed up at her brother's frustrated face. "To try to find something— anything that might help him track the killer."

"Someone must have followed you," he said grimly.

She shivered at the thought. "We weren't aware that anyone was around," she told him. "We'd been out there for a long time, searching up and down the arroyo. We'd decided to go up top and while we were up there Jess said—"

She broke off as she suddenly remembered the way

he'd looked before the shot rang out. He'd been smiling at her. Really smiling.

"Jess said what?" Ross urged her to go on.

Shaking her head, she swallowed at the lump of tears burning her throat. "That he wanted to talk to me about something. So we got off our horses and that's when the shooting happened. Now I might not ever know what he was going to say!"

Ross soberly studied his sister's face. "Not too long ago you swore to me that you'd gotten over Jess Hastings. But I was right when I told the nurse you were in love with him. Wasn't I?"

She nodded sadly. "For a long time I tried to convince myself I was over Jess. But he came back and the moment I saw him it was like nothing had ever changed," she whispered hoarsely.

Ross's expression was both sorrowful and perplexed. "I can't imagine what it must feel like to love someone that much."

"Oh Ross, I have money and a successful medical practice. But none of it means anything without Jess. He's all I've ever needed or wanted in life."

Regret spilled through her and stained her heart with bleakness. Why hadn't she told Jess all that, she asked herself. Why had she held back and tried to pretend she wasn't dying inside without him? Now it might be too late.

Ross patted her cheek. "For what it's worth, Jess is a tough SOB. If anybody can pull out of this, he can."

Victoria's gaze went over to the object of their discussion and she was suddenly shocked to see Jess staring straight at the two of them.

"As soon as I get out of this bed, Ketchum, I'll give you a taste of just how tough."

Chapter Fifteen

The groggily spoken words were the most beautiful sound Victoria had ever heard.

"Jess! Oh thank God, you're awake!" Victoria exclaimed as she rushed to his bedside.

Following at a slower pace, Ross stood beside his sister and grinned sheepishly at the undersheriff. "That part about the SOB was meant in a nice kind of way, Jess."

Jess tried to muster up a grin, but all he could manage was to lift one corner of his lips. "I meant what I said in a nice kind of way, too."

Weakly, he motioned to the insulated pitcher sitting on a nearby portable table. "Is that water? My throat feels like I've been trying to swallow a handful of cotton balls."

Victoria moved around the bed and poured a plastic

glass full of water, then held it carefully to his lips. He drank thirstily, all the while his gray eyes were focused on Victoria's face.

"What happened?" he asked once she set the glass aside and he'd regained his breath.

Ross cast a proud glance at his sister. "Victoria saved your life. That's what happened."

Ignoring her brother's comment, Victoria touched a hand to Jess's warm forehead. "You don't remember?"

A frown furrowed his brow as he tried to put the wheels of his memory into motion. "I remember going after Chito and then I heard a loud noise like a shot."

Her gaze went to his heavily bandaged shoulder and his eyes dawned with the shock and realization of what she was telling him.

"I'm afraid you're right, Jess," she said gently. "There was a shot. I'm not sure from which direction. I do know it was loud. And from the damage the bullet caused to your shoulder, I'd say it had to have been fired from a rifle."

He drew in a long, ragged breath and let it out. "I wonder who the hell wants me dead?"

"Don't think about it," she said softly. "Sheriff Perez and Deputy Redwing are working on that question right now. So all you need to do is concentrate on getting well."

With a smile of relief, she glanced over to Ross. "Would you go down to the nurses' station and let them know Jess is awake?"

Grinning broadly, he headed toward the door. "Sure, sis. I've been trying to think of a reason to introduce myself to the little redhead down there. You just gave me a good one.''

Rolling her eyes, she asked, ''Since when did you need a reason?''

Waving away her question, Ross made a quick exit from the room and Victoria turned her full attention back to Jess. He seemed to be watching her with a hunger she'd never seen before and she wondered if the knock on his head had done something to his thinking.

''How does your head feel?'' she asked.

A tight grimace came over his face as his hand came up to touch the bandage near his left temple. ''It hurts like hell. What happened to it? Was I shot twice?''

''No. You fell backward into the ravine. Your head must have hit a rock.''

Groaning with disbelief, he closed his eyes. ''Dear God, what happened out there anyway? Were you shot at, too?''

Except for the shadow of beard along his chin and jaw, his face was so pale. Just seeing him in such a vulnerable condition made her heart ache to hold him, to take away his pain.

''No. After you fell, there were no more shots.''

''You could have been killed, Victoria,'' he gently chastised. ''You should have gotten on Dixie and hightailed it out of there.''

His eyes flew open and settled soberly on her face. Even now, it scared the hell out of him to think of her out there on that lonely range, a sitting target for the gunman. Just knowing she'd put her life in danger in order to save his, humbled Jess like nothing ever had. "Ross said you saved my life."

Uncomfortable with the idea of being labeled a heroine, Victoria's gaze fell to the white sheet covering his chest. "Ross is exaggerating. All I did was tend your wounds as best I could. I didn't have much to work with."

His gray eyes drifted to her shirt where the bottom half had been ripped away for bandages. "I see," he said wryly.

Blushing, she glanced down to where part of her midriff was exposed. At the same time, she touched a hand to her tangled hair. "I haven't had a chance to go home and change. I must look a real mess."

"You look like an angel to me," he said in a voice rough with emotion.

Lifting her eyes to his, she tried to smile, but it was hard to do with tears threatening to overtake her.

"How long have you been here?" he asked.

She glanced toward the window where the full light of morning was now streaming through the blinds. "All night."

"My grandparents and Katrina—"

"Were here," she interrupted. "I sent them home with a promise I would call them as soon as you woke up. I guess I should do that now."

She reached for the phone on the nightstand, but Jess caught her hand midway.

"Later," he said.

Her brows lifted. "They're very worried about you, Jess."

"You can call them in a few minutes," he promised, then gestured toward the bedrail separating the two of them. "Can you lower this damn thing?"

She put down the metal rail while eyeing him guardedly. "If you're having ideas of getting up, forget them. You're much too weak."

The sudden glint in his eyes said he'd like to prove her wrong. In more ways than just standing on his feet.

"I'm not going to try that. Not yet anyway," he told her, then patted the tiny space of empty mattress at his side. "Come here and sit. I want you close to me."

She regarded him skeptically. "I've already had a squabble with your nurse. If the doctor comes in here and finds me on your bed, we'll have him to deal with."

Jess took her by the hand and pulled her down beside him. "The only doctor I want to deal with is this one," he said huskily.

She groaned as her heart began to melt at his touch. "Jess, if you're—"

"I'm trying to talk to you," he interrupted. "That was my intention last night at the arroyo, but the gunfire stopped me."

"And nearly killed you in the process!" she exclaimed.

His features hardened with determination. "The coward who tried to dry gulch me is going to get his due, Victoria. I'm going to see to that."

Her resolve to be cool and collected in front of him crumpled and tears began to trickle down her face. "Oh Jess, I thought—when I saw you lying at the bottom of the arroyo—I was so afraid you were dead!''

Pain from his shoulder caused him to wince as he lifted a hand to her wet cheek. ''I don't know why you would care,'' he said, his gruff voice filled with self-disgust. ''I've been a bastard to you.''

Shock widened her eyes and parted her lips. ''No! Jess—''

He shook his head as regret marred his features. ''You know it's true, Tori. All those years ago—I should have never forced you to choose between me and Tucker. It was wrong—selfish of me. I—''

She reached for his hands and clutched them tight. ''Oh Jess, it wasn't wrong. You wanted to be your own man. I should have respected that. I should have gone with you to Texas.''

A look of awe came over his face. ''I think you actually mean that.''

''Why shouldn't I mean it? I've certainly had a long time to think about it. Over four long years. Do you know how many times I've wondered how things would have turned out for us if I'd not been so stubborn and gone with you to El Paso?'' Anguish filled her eyes as her head swung back and forth with sorrow. ''It's no wonder you can't forgive me.''

With a great groan, he pulled his hands from her grasp and attempted to push himself up to a sitting position.

''Jess!'' Concerned for his wounds, she reached to help him. ''What do you think you're doing? You—''

Her words broke off with a stunned little ''oh'' as he enveloped her in his arms and pressed her head against the middle of his chest. "I'm trying to tell you that I love you, Tori. I don't guess I've ever stopped."

The admission numbed her with shock, and for a moment all she could do was listen to the precious beat of his heart. Then slowly she lifted her head to look at him. "I never thought I would ever hear those words from you, Jess. You said you would never love another woman. You said—"

"Damn it, Victoria, I said a lot of things. Things I didn't mean. Because you hurt me. And I wanted you to think—I wanted myself to think—that I didn't care—that I was perfectly happy living without you."

Unable to allow herself to believe, to hope this all wasn't just a dream, she began to stroke his arm. "Jess, you've had trauma to your head—"

"I've had trauma to my *heart*."

"When a person has a brush with death," she continued to rationalize, "it works on his mind, his thinking. It's perfectly normal for you to get all emotional. Especially toward someone whom you believe saved your life. But later—"

His hand gave her shoulder a little shake. "Listen to me, you stubborn little thing. This has nothing to do with me being shot. Last night on the T Bar K, when I told you I wanted to talk to you—*this* is what it was about. You and me. And the fact that I can't go on like this."

As she tried to assemble everything he'd just said, her lips parted, her eyes widened with the dawning realization. "You mean, last night before all this happened, you were going to tell me you loved me?"

Frowning, his hands came up to cradle her face. "I know it all sounds crazy. But—"

"Crazy? It sounds a little late to me! What were you waiting on?"

He sighed. "The perfect time, I suppose. But I guess I waited until it was almost too late." He paused, his eyes desperately searching her face. "Or maybe it's already too late. Maybe you don't give a damn how I feel anymore."

Suddenly all the pain and hopelessness she'd gone through for the past four years flooded out of her heart. Tears sprang to her eyes. "I've been trying to tell myself I didn't care. But I haven't been doing a very good job of it, Jess. The moment I saw you again at the ranch, I knew that nothing had changed for me. I loved you madly four years ago. And I still do."

Groaning with relief, he pressed her head against his good shoulder. "Oh Victoria, I don't know why I deserve you. I don't know why you would still love me. But I thank God that you do."

Moving her head, she pressed a kiss against his neck and then his cheek. "I still don't understand, Jess. If it wasn't the shooting, what made you change your mind about us?"

His hands meshed into her tangled hair and tilted her head so that he could look into her eyes. The love she saw on his face melted her heart with happiness and filled her whole being with glorious sunshine.

"Do you really think that was just sex we shared those nights on the T Bar K?" he asked.

"You said that's all it was."

Amusement dimpled his pale cheeks. "I must be a damn good actor if you believed that. You made me lose my head and my heart all over again, woman." His expression turned sober. "And then when you told me about the baby, I felt so sick, so cheated. I wanted to take all that pain back from you. I wanted to love you. To start all over and make it right again. But I was afraid to tell you how I felt. Afraid that you wouldn't believe me or even care.''

"Oh Jess, couldn't you guess how I felt about you? Couldn't you see? Those nights we made love—they were so precious to me—and I tried to show you how I felt—but you were so cold, I was afraid to say the words to you. Afraid you would reject me like you did so long ago.''

Groaning, he leaned forward and kissed her with a tenderness that brought fresh tears to her eyes.

"I've made some mistakes that hurt us both, Tori. Especially marrying Regina. I had the stupid notion she would make me forget that I was miserable without you. But she realized right off that my heart was never in our marriage. It was no surprise to either of us that it failed almost as fast as it began.''

Her fingertips stroked his face. "At least she gave you a child.''

Remorse twisted his lips. "Do you regret that, Victoria? That I have a child?''

"Oh no," she assured him, then to underscore just how much she meant it, she gave him a generous smile. "I love Katrina. And I hope this means you're going to give me the chance to be her mother.''

Catching her hand, he placed a kiss upon her palm, then turned his attention to her face where he proceeded to kiss her cheeks, her chin and finally her lips.

"It's my deepest wish that you'll be her mother and that we can give her brothers and sisters," he murmured in a voice rough with emotion.

With a little moan of joy, Victoria flung her arm around his neck and pressed her cheek against his. "Now you're talking my kind of language, lawman."

"When are you going to marry me?"

Incredible joy swept her up and brought laughter to her lips. "As soon as you can get out of this bed."

He responded with a sexy chuckle. "I'll try my best to be out of here by tonight."

She pulled her head back so that she could give him a stern look of warning. "Not hardly. You've got to rest and mend first."

His eyes twinkled as he grinned at her. "Aw, you're no fun at all, Doc."

And he was, she realized with aching happiness, the same Jess who'd once charmed and thrilled her, the same man she planned to love for the rest of her life.

Her hands came up to frame his face. "Darling, it won't be long. And when you do get out of here, I'm going to show you how very much I love you."

"Mmm. And I'm going to hold you to that promise," he whispered against her lips.

They were sealing their plan with a kiss when a knock on the door interrupted them.

Frowning, Jess eased his head back from hers and called, "Come in."

Expecting the visitor to be Dr. Wallis, Victoria was surprised when she glanced over her shoulder and spotted Deputy Redwing entering the room.

Cradling the black Stetson in his hands, the younger man stepped up to the end of Jess's bed.

After a silent nod of greeting to Victoria, he turned his attention to Jess. "I just got the news from Ross that you were awake. I hope I'm not disturbing you."

Jess exchanged a tender look with Victoria before he turned a tired grin on the deputy. "You are. But it's good to see you anyway."

The deputy studied Jess as though he were seeing a different man from the one he worked with every day. "You sure look happy for a man who was just shot and nearly murdered."

Jess's gaze strayed lovingly back Victoria. "It's not often a man has a beautiful woman agree to marry him. You can be the first to congratulate me, Redwing."

Surprise flickered over the deputy's face as he looked from Jess to Victoria, then his features suddenly locked into an uncomfortable grimace.

"What's the matter, Daniel?" Jess joked. "Are you jealous or something?"

The deputy's gaze fell to the toes of his boots. "No. I'm very happy to hear you two have finally mended your fences. There's something else—"

Pausing, he awkwardly cleared his throat and lifted his troubled gaze back to the newly engaged couple.

Sensing that something was terribly wrong, Victoria's worried gaze flew to Jess's.

"All right," Jess demanded. "What's wrong?"

The other man heaved out a heavy breath. "We've been out searching the spot where you were shot."

Victoria watched Jess's jaw tighten and suddenly Marina's words of warning were racing through her mind. *Someone will be hurt again.* Had the cook really known?

Impatient now, Jess made a gesture for him to spit out the rest of his news.

Redwing said, "We found the rifle that was fired

at you. It was on the other side of the gorge behind juniper bush.''

Jess and Victoria exchanged excited glances.

"That's great news, isn't it?'' she asked eagerly.

"Damn right,'' Jess told her. Beaming now, h looked at his chief deputy. "I take it you've run th serial numbers and come up with the owner of th rifle.''

Redwing nodded glumly as, once again, he tossed a troubled glance at Victoria. "Yes sir, I'm afraid w have.''

"Afraid hell,'' Jess fired back at him. "Who is the bastard?''

The deputy drew in a long breath and let it out. "Ross Ketchum.''

The name fell like a bomb in the quiet room.

Reeling from the repercussion, Victoria reached for Jess's hand. He squeezed her fingers and his warm reassurance told her they were going to face this thing together, the same way they were going to face the rest of their lives.

*　*　*　*　*

Could Victoria's brother be a killer?
Look for Ross's story,
HIS DEFENDER, only from Stella Bagwell—
Silhouette Special Edition,
coming in December 2003
as, MEN OF THE WEST *continues!*

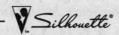

SPECIAL EDITION™

MONTANA MAVERICKS

The Kingsleys

**Nothing is as it seems
beneath the big skies of Montana.**

HER MONTANA MILLIONAIRE
by **Crystal Green**
(Silhouette Special Edition #1574)

New York socialite Jinni Fairchild was barely surviving Rumor's
slow pace. Until she met Max Cantrell. Tall. Dark. Gorgeous.
And rich as Midas. Would his unhurried sensuality tempt this
fast-lane girl to stop and smell the roses—with him?

Available November 2003 at your favorite retail outlet.

Your opinion is important to us! Please take a few moments to share your thoughts with us about your experiences with Harlequin and Silhouette books. ...ur comments will be very useful in ensuring that we deliver books you love to read.

Please take a few minutes to complete the questionnaire, then send it to us at the address below.

Send your completed questionnaires to:
Harlequin/Silhouette Reader Survey, P.O. Box 9046, Buffalo, NY 14269-9046

...As you may know, there are many different lines under the Harlequin and Silhouette ...brands. Each of the lines is listed below. Please check the box that most represents ...your reading habit for each line.

Line	Currently read this line	Do not read this line	Not sure if I read this line
...arlequin American Romance	❏	❏	❏
...arlequin Duets	❏	❏	❏
...arlequin Romance	❏	❏	❏
...arlequin Historicals	❏	❏	❏
...arlequin Superromance	❏	❏	❏
...arlequin Intrigue	❏	❏	❏
...arlequin Presents	❏	❏	❏
...arlequin Temptation	❏	❏	❏
...arlequin Blaze	❏	❏	❏
...ilhouette Special Edition	❏	❏	❏
...ilhouette Romance	❏	❏	❏
...ilhouette Intimate Moments	❏	❏	❏
...ilhouette Desire	❏	❏	❏

2. Which of the following best describes why you bought *this book?* One answer only, please.

the picture on the cover	❏	the title	❏
the author	❏	the line is one I read often	❏
part of a miniseries	❏	saw an ad in another book	❏
saw an ad in a magazine/newsletter	❏	a friend told me about it	❏
I borrowed/was given this book	❏	other: _____	❏

3. Where did you buy *this book?* One answer only, please.

at Barnes & Noble	❏	at a grocery store	❏
at Waldenbooks	❏	at a drugstore	❏
at Borders	❏	on eHarlequin.com Web site	❏
at another bookstore	❏	from another Web site	❏
at Wal-Mart	❏	Harlequin/Silhouette Reader	❏
at Target	❏	Service/through the mail	
at Kmart	❏	used books from anywhere	❏
at another department store or mass merchandiser	❏	I borrowed/was given this book	❏

4. On average, how many Harlequin and Silhouette books do you buy at one time?

I buy _____ books at one time ❏
I rarely buy a book ❏

MRQ403SSE-1A

5. How many times per month do you shop for any *Harlequin and/or Silhouette* bo[…]
One answer only, please.

1 or more times a week	❑	a few times per year
1 to 3 times per month	❑	less often than once a year
1 to 2 times every 3 months	❑	never

6. When you think of your ideal heroine, which *one* statement describes her the be[…]
One answer only, please.

She's a woman who is strong-willed	❑	She's a desirable woman
She's a woman who is needed by others	❑	She's a powerful woman
She's a woman who is taken care of	❑	She's a passionate woman
She's an adventurous woman	❑	She's a sensitive woman

7. The following statements describe types or genres of books that you may be
interested in reading. Pick *up to 2 types* of books that you are most interested in.

I like to read about truly romantic relationships
I like to read stories that are sexy romances
I like to read romantic comedies
I like to read a romantic mystery/suspense
I like to read about romantic adventures
I like to read romance stories that involve family
I like to read about a romance in times or places that I have never seen
Other: _____

*The following questions help us to group your answers with those readers who are
similar to you. Your answers will remain confidential.*

8. Please record your year of birth below.
19 ____

9. What is your marital status?
single ❑   married ❑   common-law ❑   widowed ❑
divorced/separated ❑

10. Do you have children 18 years of age or younger currently living at home?
yes ❑   no ❑

11. Which of the following best describes your employment status?
employed full-time or part-time ❑   homemaker ❑   student ❑
retired ❑   unemployed ❑

12. Do you have access to the Internet from either home or work?
yes ❑   no ❑

13. Have you ever visited eHarlequin.com?
yes ❑   no ❑

14. What state do you live in?
_____

15. Are you a member of Harlequin/Silhouette Reader Service?
yes ❑   Account # _____   no ❑   MRQ403SSE-1B

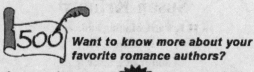

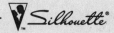

#1573 A LITTLE BIT PREGNANT—Susan Mallery
Readers' Ring

Security expert Zane Rankin could have any woman he wanted.. and often did. Computer hacker and wallflower Nicki Beauman had contented herself with being platonic with her sexy friend Za Until one night of unbridled—and unexpected—passion changed their relationship forever….

#1574 HER MONTANA MILLIONAIRE—Crystal Green
Montana Mavericks: The Kingsleys

Sunday driving through life was billionaire and single dad Max Cantrell's way. Celebrity biographer Jinni Fairchild preferre living in the fast lane. But when these two opposites collided, ther was nothing but sparks! Could they overcome the detours keeping them apart?

#1575 PRINCE OF THE CITY—Nikki Benjamin
Manhattan Multiples

When the city's mayor threatened to sever funds for Eloise Vale's nonprofit organization, she reacted like a mama bear protecting he cubs. But mayor Bill Harper was her one-time love. Eloise would fight for Manhattan Multiples, but could she resist the lure of her sophisticated ex and protect herself from falling for her enemy?

#1576 MAN IN THE MIST—Annette Broadrick
Secret Sisters

Gregory Dumas was searching for a client's long-lost family— he'd long ago given up looking for love. But in chaste beauty Fiona MacDonald he found both. Would this wary P.I. give in to the feelings Fiona evoked? Or run from the heartache he was certain would follow…?

#1577 THE CHRISTMAS FEAST—Peggy Webb
Dependable had never described Jolie "Kat" Coltrane. But zany and carefree Kat showed her family she was a responsible adult by cooking Christmas dinner—with the help of one unlikely holiday guest. Lancelot Estes, a hardened undercover agent, was charmed by the artless Kat…and soon the two were cooking up more than dinner!

#1578 A MOTHER'S REFLECTION—Elissa Ambrose
Drama teacher Rachel Hartwell's latest role would be her most important yet: befriending her biological daughter. When Rachel learned that the baby she'd given up for adoption years ago had lost her adoptive mother, she vowed to become a part of her daughter's life. But did that include falling in love with Adam Wessler—her child's adoptive father?